Stairs to Yonder

MARY FLOWERS CARTER

ALSO BY MARY FLOWERS CARTER

Sweet Peppers - Sour Grapes & Wild Flowers

Lest We Forget

A New Birth

Streets of Ferry

(a sequel to *Lest We Forget*)

Stairs to Yonder

DEDICATION

This book is dedicated to my four grandchildren:
Maryssa, Charles, Alonzo and Carter.

MEMORY

I write this book in loving memory of my daddy and mama:
George and Emma.

"Research shows that there is only half as much variation in student achievement between schools as there is among classrooms in the same school. If you want your child to get the best education possible, it is actually more important to get him assigned to a great teacher than to a great school."

~ Bill Gates

FORWARD

Education is defined as the attainment of additional knowledge, skills, or teachings. These skill sets allow the participants to have some competency that they did not possess at the beginning of the process.

African-Americans have seen the value of this process since we have come to the shores of North America. Early learning took place through *"watching and mimicking"* what we saw. Some were fortunate enough to be "taught in secret" by our "owners" (in slavery). Those on the forefront took measures to establish schools (often known as "colored schools") since initially we were not allowed to attend "all white" schools. Separate but equal was "fought" and overturned on the educational front in the court case "Brown v. Board of Education" (1954). We acknowledged the value of education so greatly that we endured many hardships to insure "our people" had the opportunity to make these practices a realization.

Our historically black colleges and universities (HBCU) are just an extension of this process. With the establishment of **Cheyney University of Pennsylvania** in 1837 and our own alma maters **North Carolina Agricultural and Technical State University** in 1890 and **Slater Industrial Academy** in 1892, now known as **Winston-Salem State University**, this legacy is still represented today. We celebrate, cultivate and value these institutions and others like them across the country.

Fast forward to today, we need to continue to nurture and support education, not taking for granted what our ancestors endured for us to have these experiences.

We don't...

Charletta Carter Armstrong, MD
Graduate of North Carolina Agricultural and Technical State University
Daphne Carter Wright, MBA, PHR, SHRM-CP
Graduate of Winston-Salem State University

ACKNOWLEDGEMENTS

First and foremost, I thank God for enabling me to write another novel, my fifth one.

I would like to extend my love and gratitude to all the wonderful people who supported and inspired me over the years. My husband, Charles Carter, was not only supportive and inspirational, but he sustained me, while cooking the most delicious, nutritious meals.

I owe my largest debt to my extraordinary, first-rate editor, Melinda Willms. With her keen editorial eyes, she cleared the underbrush and provided much literary knowledge. Over the years, she has become my agent/editor and friend. Her friendship and knowledge of the arts were indispensable and will be unforgettable.

Deep appreciation goes to my friends and sorority sisters, for their love and support, and for nurturing me at a time when I really needed encouragement.

Writing this book became a family affair, when my eldest daughter, Daphne Carter Wright, assisted me with her computer knowledge, and also made literary contributions. Her expert judgment and critical analysis were invaluable. My younger daughter, Dr. Charletta Carter Armstrong, had vision and faith in me. She became my doctor on call, both mentally and physically, while providing me with much infinite medical knowledge.

Finally, I am grateful for my grandkids, who were always upbeat. When I needed it the most, they took my mind off my work, and helped me to relax.

STAIRS TO YONDER

Sequel to

Streets of Ferry

PROLOGUE

Be there as it may, no word in Webster's Dictionary had more meaning for Joey Bloomfield than the word, *depression*.

On one hand, there was the *Great Depression* of 1920-1940. That period of time was not only referred to as the Great Depression, but it was also known as the Hoover Depression and Hoover Days. In the eyes of the middle class and the poor, President Herbert Hoover was thought of as a poor leader, a weak president, and an all-around awful politician. The multitudes were ill-fed and poorly clad. The great and sad irony was that the poor had lived a depressed life before "The Depression" was officially recognized and given its many titles.

In the un-calm and stormy time, there was a reduction of the tax "burden" on the rich by means of the combination of shrunken economy and repeated tax increases from the passage of the Tax Act in 1932. It was apparent that these taxes soaked the poor. The rich were prepared to face the hectic times the Great Depression wrought with equanimity, and even saw it as a potentially healthy development. The middle class and poor assumed the wealthy personally were in agreement and thought of the tax increases as a solution to the problem, while they paid the price for the extravagance.

The mal-distribution of income between the rich and poor grew, while the wealthy continually got richer, and the poor got poorer. Government policies during the time were designed to achieve just that end. The unfavorable climate for the labor unions made it more difficult for workers to obtain their share of the benefits of rising productivity. Even the stock market reacted with its "great, sensitive brain," and was as uncertain as the weather.

In the waning years of the Great Depression, as the economy further deteriorated and the social fabric of the country continued to fray, the people who had been left behind by the political and economic powers that be understandably believed the worst about the government and its respective agencies.

Then, the New Deal came about in 1936 under President Franklin Delano Roosevelt (FDR). For men like Joey Bloomfield, the most important aspect of the New Deal was the Works Progress Administration. The program gave them hope, while they referred to the job as the WPA. They had been jobless and had been searching for work in vain for so long. Former jobless men were heard making comments such as, "It makes me feel like an American citizen to be able to earn my own living again." "Without work, life seems so empty, and the supplied funds are not enough to live decent on." "Give a man a dole, and you save his body and destroy his spirit, but give him a job and you will save both body and spirit."

After 18 years of marriage, there was a sudden "mental depression" that appeared in the Bloomfield's household. Joey's wife, Amma, was attacked by anxiety disorders after the delivery of her 6th child. The family members were oblivious to the real problem and had mistaken beliefs that she would come around in a few days. Due to the stigma surrounding mental illness, she and the family suffered more than was necessary. After weeks of living in a difficult situation, Amma's parents took matters into their hands and took her into their home. The Jamisons (Joey's in-laws), took a spiritual approach to life. They believed in a Higher Power, and when the illness appeared insoluble, despite all their best efforts, they turned everything over to God. Faith enabled them to let go of the idea that they had to fully control everything.

When Joey first realized that his life had greatly changed, he felt distressed and believed that the bad event was brutal. His dear, love one and wife was not in the home, and he was left with the children and teenagers. With the help of God above, Mr. Hartman was there to assist him. Over the years, the white man and he had given assistance to each other. They both contributed to each other to further their progress and, or advancements. Hartman had dealt with mental illness and was ready to assist.

Joey developed his spirituality and came to the realization that there was a larger purpose in life beyond the overt appearance of what had happened to him and his family. He believed that, what seemed like an unfair situation would have some greater meaning or purpose in a broader scheme of things. While gaining experience over a period of time, he embraced life with optimisms.

Amma had her way of coping with the unpredictable and the unforeseen. She prayed continually and believed that her prayers would make things better. She would quote the popular phrases: *Prayers change things*; *God knows what's best for us*; and, *everything happens for a reason.*

Stairs to Yonder is the sequel to the original novel, **Streets of Ferry**, the continuing life experiences of the Bloomfield family. The family is taking their umpteenth trip across Streets of Ferry. The time is right for them to return to their own home in Jasper. After returning, the Bloomfields will begin building their stairs to yonder.

CONTENTS

1 CHAPTER ONE

JOEY

"No man succeeds without a good woman

behind him, wife or mother.

If it is both, he is twice

blessed indeed."

~ Godfrey Winn

Amma quietly hummed, "When the Roll is Called up Yonder." She was carrying a little more weight than she had when we were first married, but I still thought of her as nothing short of beauty with her stiff starched apron tightly tied about her round body. Even at her age, she had no wrinkles in her caramel colored face. She was so deep in her thoughts that she didn't seem to recognize my presence.

I stood in my low hanging overalls, scratching my head. I think we were thinking along the same line. *"How could it be that we had only three out of five children still at home?"* Of course, Ida Lee had finished high school and gone off to live with her Aunt Maggie, where she found a job working as a bus girl at the Hot Shoppe in Bethesda, Maryland, a wealthy neighborhood that was. At that restaurant, colored people were not allowed to be waiters or waitresses, and it was unheard of to be the receptionist or greeter. Our daughter had a good work ethics, seemed happy, and knew how to budget her few pennies.

Her aunt was a staunch member of the Church of God. She was a generous person who was endowed with a good sense of humor. Ida Lee had adjusted well. She had grown up under the morals and practices of the church and did not have to undergo many changes. All of her letters to us carried much excitement about all the activities and various groups of interests in the church. She seemed to be surrounded by beautiful people—not wealthy—but well endowed. She did not mention anything that was undesirable.

On the other hand, our son, Buddy, seemed unhappy on the farm with his uncle. When we visited, we noticed that his eyes were filled with sadness, and he seldom smiled. My heart cracked, and I felt pity as I observed him sitting alone without mingling among us. Did he blame us for his unhappiness?

As I stood thinking, Amma turned from the clothes line and noticed that I was watching her. She said, "I been watching for the mailman, 'cause Ida Lee should be writing letting us know if she's coming home for Christmas."

I asked, "You think she saved that much money?"

"Yeah, she knows how to save her pennies. I'm so glad Maggie isn't charging her any rent."

"Yeah, she sho' good to her," I commented, as I decided to help Amma finish hanging the clothes on the line. She wanted the clothes hung a certain way and didn't trust me to hang them. Instead of just watching her do her perfect job, I would get them out of the basket and hand them to her. If I did not give them to her in the order that she desired to hang them, she would adjust by skipping a space.

Still thinking about Buddy, I said, "It would sho' be nice if Buddy would write us."

"Sho' would be, but ain't no need to even think about that," Amma said. As she quit hanging out clothes, looked at me with her beautiful brown eyes and commented, "I wonder if Buddy know how to write a letter."

"I don't know," I said, thinking back about how he refused

to do his homework. Mae Etta tried to do it for him, but sometimes, he wouldn't tell her what to do. Then I said, "Buddy didn't talk too much 'bout school work."

"Lawd, he sho' didn't," Amma exclaimed, as she stood with her hands propped on her hips.

I took a quick breath and added, "He didn't care too much 'bout school, anyway."

"Didn't care nothin' 'bout it. Wanted to get away from it," Amma said, as she went back to hanging clothes.

I had other things to do; so, I left the clothes hanging to Amma. There were many other things to do around the house.

My wife and I continued to trade confidential words when we were alone at home. We spoke about having to send Buddy to stay with an uncle who could have more control over him, and when we did, Amma's tears fell like rain. Despite our sadness, we realized we had nothing constructive for Buddy to do. Furthermore, we had already done too much haggling and negotiating in our home. Amma was the strict disciplinarian, and so was her brother. We guessed that our son did not appreciate that kind of living, but after careful consideration, we decided to let well enough do.

The day was glorious, and the wind was blowing its first dead leaves from the oaks. It was the fall of 1956 when a letter appeared in our mailbox, postmarked: Washington, D.C. The free-swinging cursive writing on the blue envelope gave us a hint---a letter from our daughter. Hallelujah!!!

Getting mail was one of the thrills of the day for our family; however, most of the time I was not at home to receive the mail. Amma had her own way of opening an envelope. She gently tore down the side of the envelope, gave the side a puff of air, and then, removed the letter. Happiness was shining in our eyes, and an uncontrollable joy weighed on my chest, as we all waited for her to read the letter aloud. Finally, Amma read:

Dear Mommy and Daddy,

I received your letter on Tuesday. I was so happy to hear from you.

How are you and the family doing? I am well and doing fine. We are having lots of rain here in the Washington, D.C.

Aunt Maggie is well and doing fine. She sends her love. I can't wait for Christmas to come because I will be coming home. I will be bringing you all gifts. I won't tell you what I will be bringing, but I am enjoying shopping for you all. You will probably like what I am getting for each of you.

I am getting the Trail Way bus home on December 23rd and will be arriving in New Bern around 1 o'clock. Then, I will take the 3 o'clock bus out - to Jasper. Daddy, don't worry about me. I don't need anybody to pick me up in New Bern.

See you soon.

Yours truly,

Ida Lee

When she finished reading, the letter was passed around, and everyone read for himself, while Amma got up and went straight to the kitchen calendar to mark the date and time of Ida Lee's arrival.

After hearing from Ida Lee that fall day, I worked all afternoon around Sam Riddick's house. I was feeling more adequate and worked late into the night after returning home. The axe was not as heavy, and the mosquitoes' bites were not as sharp. Dragging wood to the woodpile seemed easier. All cares seemed to have taken flight, as if they were now floating far above me, in the kind blue sky, with the shining moon and twinkling stars.

Later, I went to bed with a smile on my face; and when the sun peeked through the blinds the next morning, I jumped out of bed, quickly got into my same old, patched, monkey backs, slipped into my overly mended socks, and put my ashy feet into my rusty shoes. Gathering lighter splinters from our wood box in back of the stove, and then piling on the logs, a fire was soon blazing. The brewing coffee's aroma soon found its way through the house.

Later, I sat at the table and sipped my usual first cup of Five O'clock coffee while daydreaming about my children. Ida Lee, the oldest, was safe with her aunt and other relatives in the city, and I was feeling pretty good about her situation.

Now, at this point in my life, another child is leaving our household. Mae Etta would graduate from high school in the spring of next year, and she had always talked about being a school teacher. I was really bothered about the fact that I did not have the money to send her off to college, but she didn't seem worried, and was taking other steps towards her goal. Despite the fact that my daughter felt that working in tobacco was despicable, she was considering doing the job for the summer to save money for school. We all disliked the filthy scum that stuck to the skin, and we were well aware of the low wages, and the deprivation that came with that kind of work, but somehow, we made it through many summers.

Then there was Buddy, who gave us the blues when he was at home, but we made sure that he was in a safe place. Of course, I often thought about what I could or should have done. But, the good thing was - the remaining two children, Robert and Christine, would be at home for a while.

Amma and I took a routine walk through our garden. Knowing that my oldest daughter was coming home soon made the garden seems all the more greener and the whole world felt like a brighter place to live. Harvesting time had come, and the beans and peas had dried enough to be stored. The white potatoes plants had lost their blossoms and were waiting to be dug. The shriveled-up sweet potatoes vines gave signs that they were ready for digging and banking.

Thoughts of the summer raced through my mind. My vegetable garden had given me a full workout when I fought with the weeds and grass that had tried to take over. Watching the metamorphosis of the peas, beans, greens, potatoes, fruit trees, and much more was enlightening, and made the thought of harvest time a pleasure.

I was wondering if Amma was going to do any canning this

fall. So, I asked her if she felt well enough to do any canning.

Amma stopped in her tracks and bobbed her head as she said, "Yeah, I want to do some canning this year. Been a while, but I'm feeling pretty good."

"You sho'?" I asked.

"Can't let all these fruits and vegetables go to waste," Amma announced.

"Well, you and Mae Etta do yo' best, and I'll help when I'm done at Sam's place. He is ailing; he needs me, and I need the money," I said with a chuckle.

Amma pursed her lips as she said, "Joey, you try to do too much. Let us take care of the canning."

She spoke with such tenderness, that once again I felt that she was right. So, I drifted off to the other part of the garden.

Amma caught up with me and shot me a look. I must admit, I was tempted to move to another spot. Instead, I took a deep breath, blew my nose, and while returning the handkerchief to my pocket, I said, "If we want to make it through the winter, we'll have to save all we can."

I suppose Amma suppressed a laugh and only smiled as she answered, "Lawd knows we do."

Over the week, the sky burred blue while white clouds floated overhead. I plowed up sweet potatoes and put them in piles. When the heaps hit their apexes, needles that had gathered from beneath the pine trees were used to cover the potatoes. Then the planks were nestled close to the layer of straw, forming tepees. Swinging doors made from planks made the little conical piles look like small houses standing in a row.

My happiness, already enormous, grew even greater as I noticed Amma's face, glowing with peace and joy when I entered the house. The aroma of fruits and vegetables propelled from the kitchen and swept through the entire house. Numerous jars of canned goods were mounting on the smokehouse shelves, but we felt that there was never too much for winter. With the news that our daughter would be home for a few weeks, we really tried to show off.

Seemingly, Mae Etta was busy keeping Christine happy and out of the way of Amma's work.

My Amma had breakfast ready, and I sat my long slender body down to fried salt fatback, mashed potatoes, eggs, and hot biscuits. We had too much on our minds to speak, so we ate in silence. I had my second cup of coffee before I was ready to return to the outside.

As I was leaving, Robert came into the room, and pleaded, "Daddy, I wanta' go to the garden with you. I took all the canned jars to the smokehouse and put them on the shelf. So, mama don't need me no mo' today."

I loved working by myself. I thought no one else knew how to work in my garden, but Amma gave me the eye. She had often told me that I tried to do all my gardening by myself, so I had nothing to say, but, "Reckon you kin come on out, Robert. Put on that old straw hat and yo' old patched dungarees. As I started out the door, I turned around and added, "And don't forget to put on yo' garden shoes."

Robert grinned and said, "Ok daddy! Be right out." He ran to get his hat and shoes.

Back at work in our nearly perfect garden, the corn stalks still stood with hardened corn, waiting to be gathered. I knew that we had just a few weeks to gather it before the sky would open up. Hurricane season was just around the corner.

As I looked up at the sky, the clouds seemed heavy with rain, so, I hollered to Robert, "Bring me some sacks out of the smokehouse when you come!"

I waited patiently before Robert hollered back, "Daddy, ain't no sacks in here."

Hollering back, I said, "Look in that, there old box."

"There ain't no box nowhere in here," Robert answered.

"Good Gosh, Robert, do I have walk all the way back to git them?" I hollered.

From the smokehouse, I heard, "I'm lookin'! I'm lookin'!"

My patience was wearing thin, as I craned my neck to see if he was coming out the door. When my neck became almost stiff, I hustled back to the little house, looked under some old wooden slats, pulled out the box, opened it up and there were the burlap bags. I could feel myself losing control, and almost said, "This is the reason I don't want you out here."

Keeping quiet as I should have, we put our sacks over our heads and let them hang from our shoulders. We filled them with corn, and dragged them to the smokehouse, dumping the ears on the floor in a corner near the slats. The corn would make our chickens happy, and we were hoping they would lay more eggs and give us happiness in return. Chickens, that laid eggs, had an advantage over the ones that did not. The ones, that did not bring forth eggs, had a death sentence hanging over their heads. They ended up in a pot of stew or a frying pan and finally, on our kitchen table.

The nights were getting somewhat cooler. The cool breeze was delicious as it moved the curtains. I shifted my position and rested my head on my pillow to dream a little. I thought about my wonderful family, and the fact that I would get to see my oldest daughter in a few weeks. The nights were so peaceful that in the mornings, I was ready to move on to my next mature crop. The apple trees were loaded with fruit, and the plum and pear trees' branches were almost touching the ground. No matter how much I liked to do my work without the children being in my way, Mae Etta and Robert decided that they wanted to go fruit picking with me. They exuded much happiness as they said in unison, "Daddy, we wanta go fruit picking with you."

I didn't answer right away, then I asked, "Do y'all know how to pick fruit?"

Together, they answered, "Oh, Yeah!"

"When did you learn?" I asked.

Mae Etta answered very quickly, "We been knowing."

"Been knowing, since when?" I questioned her. I was trying to make some sense out of the story.

"When we stayed at Mrs. Jones' house, she let us help her pick her fruit," Mae Etta said, as she twisted around on her heels.

"What kind a fruit did Mrs. Jones have?" I asked.

"She got apples." Robert quickly said.

"She got some peaches, too, and tomatoes an-an-an......." and Mae Etta's voice trailed off into the blue.

Without another word, I let them come along. At first, they spent more time chattering and eating than picking fruit, but when they were full, the job went pretty steady. In no time, we were carrying sacks of fruit to the kitchen for Amma to preserve.

Birds chattered like the children outside the kitchen as Amma and I hustled here and there like busy ants. We spoke of Mr. Jamison who usually distilled grapes into wine in the fall. I asked, "Do you think yo' father will have enough grapes for his wine this year? You know we have mo' than we need for preserves."

Amma looked at me with suspicious eyes, as she said, "You know me and momma don't care 'bout that wine."

I kept the teasing going, "We have left over grapes that he could use for his wine."

"We'll use our grapes for preserves," she said, without looking at me.

Amma's mother, Mrs. Jamison, never liked the idea of her husband making wine, and taught the children that drinking wine was a sin. So, my wife didn't care to dwell on the topic, but Ida Lee and Mae Etta knew about their grandfather's wine. It was my understanding that some of the young adults had shared some with them. They were to keep the secret from the older adults, but someone had let the cat out of the bag.

Our dinner was collard greens, white potatoes, sweet potatoes, and a variety of preserves with hot biscuits. Many times, we had meatless meals, but I always had my fatback on the side.

The busy day had given us all a workout, and we seemed to have had just enough energy for chewing and swallowing our food. Silence permeated the kitchen while we listened to the tick-tock of the clock. After dinner, Mae Etta cleaned the kitchen. Robert fed the dogs the leftovers before washing his feet, face, and hands for bedtime. Amma and I did our usual walk through the garden.

I asked Amma, "You thinking 'bout Buddy?"

For a while, Amma said nothing. Then, with her voice cracking, she muttered, "Reckon I am. Seems like I can't get him off my mind. Sho' wish I could do something to make him happier."

"We sho' tried to be good to him - don't you think?" I muttered.

"I don't think he's faring too bad, but then, I don't *know*," Amma said, as she propped her hands on her hips, closed her eyes, and turned her head to one side as if she was resting.

I suspected that she was thinking about our differences in discipline. Discussing how to discipline the children was the "one" thing that stood between Amma and me. We both had our strong convictions about that subject. One of us was always set off in that kind of conversation. I wasn't quite ready for a display of temper, but I took a chance and stated, "It's bad that he could not act better here at home. Then, he would be here with us."

Amma gave me her usual look and said, "I think that you could have had more control over Buddy if you would help with the chastising."

"My God, Amma, I couldn't ever use the kind of punishment that you do," I said, but I almost wanted to eat my words when she hung her head and said nothing. We then silently pulled weeds, tossing them to the side, while my mind went to Amma's kind of discipline.

Amma seemed to have had a need to punish and also seemed to get so mad. She would get her switches from one of the bushes outside and would keep them behind the head of her bed. Whenever she used them, the children seemed to have paid a price for their childhood. She would crack the stinging switch across their young skin. If the children walked away before she had finished, she'd call them back. When she finished, the children were covered with welts, and some of them were bloody. During the whipping, they would pray for mercy, and afterward, they whimpered because they dared not wail. I never knew who would be next; so, I would leave the house, and would always slam the door as loud as I could, thinking that might get Amma's attention, but it never did deter her.

Amma called my attention to the moon and stars that showed overhead, and I realized that the daylight had drifted away. I could feel the chilly air of the evening creeping in around us as we moved to the house to retire for the night.

~~~~~~~~~~

The next day, it was almost dark when I entered the door. I had spent the day at Mr. Riddick's, helping with the hog killing. We were welcomed to all the parts that the owner did not want, so I was loaded with pig's feet, tongue, chitterlings, and other inner parts. To my surprise, Sam Riddick generously gave me a smoked ham. My carry-home load was so cumbersome that he offered to take me home. Throwing my bike and bags on the back of the truck, I slid in the cab with Sam. I watched him as he carefully shifted the gears, pressing slowly on the clutch and delicately prodding the stick shift on the floor, while we moved on.

The truck crept along while he looked straight ahead as if he was unsure where he was going. I could have walked faster than he was driving. Over the last few years, he had been given citations for going too slow, but it was said that he paid off the courts. Sam did not show his abundance in material possessions, but he was known as being wealthy at the bank.

I could tell that his health was failing him, as I observed his pale skin and fading blue eyes. With tobacco lining his lips and dripping down into his beard, he informed me that he would not be doing anymore farming. It was disturbing to think of the absence of the small jobs that was always there when the construction jobs became null and void. The thought made me shudder as I said, "Maybe you could try doin' just a small amount of corn."

Sam Riddick tried to speak, but went into a coughing spell, spit up phlegm, and wiped his mouth with his shirt sleeve that was already tobacco stained. In front of me, I could see him sucking in air, and when his lungs were full, he said, "No-o-o, don't want to do no mo' farming, can't do it no mo'."

When I thought of my chicken without corn, I said, "I be here to help."

When he let his pale blue eyes drift far away without speaking, I was very much aware that his farming had become smaller and smaller, and there would be no more.

We drove by cotton fields that were ready for harvest. Picking cotton was a slow process to earn money, but I needed some cash. When times were really tight, I tried to get Ida Lee and Mae Etta to pick some cotton to help with their school supplies. The first time I took them out, Ida Lee did her best and ended the day with a decent amount of cash. Mae Etta was a complete drama queen. When she spotted a cotton worm, she screamed, "I'm scared of that big fat thing!" She lingered behind screaming, "I'm scared!"

I was working for a living and tried not to waste the precious day. Glancing back, I noticed she was looking to the sky, while a plane flew overhead. With bulging eyeballs and waving hands, she pleaded, "Please, please, come down and get me! I'm in distress! I need help! Help! Help! Help!"

I went back to rescue her, moving her along by my side, as I continued through the day. At the end of the day, Mae Etta had nothing to show for her day. Ida Lee earned her day's pay. The girls always kept the money for their very own use. Mae Etta and Ida Lee were thought of as a pair, and neither was taken to the cotton field again.

My concern was to have money for such necessities as electricity and food staples, such as flour, meal, sugar, and coffee. We never worried about someone getting sick. That was where we kept the faith . . . maybe there was a home remedy, and if there was a real emergency, Doctor Little was good at seeing us and giving us credit, which we all knew that there was no way under the sun that medical bill could ever be paid off.

As I did on most Saturdays, I thumbed a ride to town to buy some necessities. Since the weather was what anybody would have ordered, Amma accompanied me. She seemed to be her old self as she stopped to talk with the other country folk who had come into town. Crowds of people were in town, moving in and out of stores, with voices echoing up and down the streets. Even the poor were enjoying the weather and their few pennies.

I was a proud man to have my wife back and able to go shopping with me, but we had to move along. We only had a few hours to do the grocery shopping before going to the bus station. The bus left the station promptly at three o'clock. As we walked from downtown to the grocery store, Amma and I had our usual discussion.

Amma expressed her feeling about the children leaving one by one. She said, "I miss the two children that are not at home, but they do have to make a living, and they can't do it 'round here."

I then stated, "I thought Mae Etta might give up the idea of goin' to college. She knows we ain't got no money."

"Mae Etta has been talking about being a school teacher ever since she started school, and I don't think she goin' give it up now. And furthermo' you taught them the importance of a good education. Didn't you?" Amma reminded me.

"Well, I guess I did. Anyway, I'll do my best, but Lawd knows, I don't see no-o-o way," I said to Amma.

My wife was forever positive as she stated, "The Lord will make a way."

"I believe yous' right, but I don't see it just now," I said, with a frown.

"When she makes up her mind, there is no changing her. She is like that in everything she go to do." Amma said, as she cracked a smile, "You remember . . ."

Before Amma could finish, I threw up my hand and stated, "Yeah, yeah, I remember."

I wasn't in the mood to hear about the Christmas tree that Mae Etta was determined to decorate, even though she didn't have any decorations. But, she did decorate it!!!

I had promised the children that we would work on making homes for the birds when I returned from New Bern. The gourds had dried and laid waiting to be carved and hung for birdhouses. Mae Etta and Robert were ready to start building the houses.

Knowing that the children were waiting for us, we hurried in the door with the sign that read: "Colored Only." We sat and waited for the bus call. After entering the bus, we slid down the narrow aisle to the back of the bus. On that particular day, we had a few seats in the back, and they were given to our women folk. Most of the black men stood until we reached our destination.

At home, I slid the burlap sack from my back, while the children stood around for their treats. The children danced around as they received candy and cookies. Such goodies were rare in the Bloomfield's household, and the children were beside themselves. They took their goody bags outside, as we gathered the gourds from the edge of the garden. I gave careful assignments, as we knifed holes in the hard shells. The gourds were wired to the pole that crossed the top of the standing post. As always, the children laughed and played with uncontrollable joy, which impeded some of the progress. When the day had almost ended, I quickened the activity so that we could finish as the sun faded behind the trees and dark drifted in.

Time dragged on, while the subject of the day was "*Ida Lee's coming home.*" Most of us felt that we were ready for her arrival when Amma had finished sprucing up the house with red berried holly branches that we had brought in from the woods. Mae Etta wanted to decorate a Christmas tree and was not satisfied until I was dragging a cedar tree home. A bucket was filled with dirt to keep the tree steady. Mae Etta's face was lit with joy and excitement as she dramatically strung homemade chains, made from holly sprig, around the tree, finishing it off by stuffing pine cones between the branches. My daughter's knowledge of decorating was awesome.

~~~~~~~~~~

The day was gray and overcast, but we didn't care. This was the day that we had been waiting for. Everyone was out of bed early. Later, we sat at the kitchen table and Amma said a long breakfast grace, blessing the food and asking for divine assistance for her traveling daughter. The three children were overflowing with joy, and laughter rang out. They were known to get a whipping for playing during prayer, but nothing seemed to upset Amma. When she finished giving thanks, she graciously scooped eggs from the dish, dipped grits from the bowl, and then, passed the plate of biscuits around. Last, but most important, were the preserves. The children heaped them onto their hot biscuits.

Later, Christine got our attention. Apple jam covered her face, spreading to her hair. We burst into laughter, and she joined us, exposing her few front teeth.

During breakfast, a few drops of rain had fallen, but it had slacked off when the meal was finished. Amma put on her old wool sweater and went out into her flower garden. Mae Etta was left behind to clean up the kitchen. I went out to the smokehouse to get my toolbox to patch an inner tube for my bike. We tried hard to occupy ourselves while waiting for the bus to come in the afternoon.

The time ticked away very slowly and seemed to have stopped on every hour. At three o'clock, the Trail Way bus stopped, the door flew open, and Ida Lee emerged, wearing a beautiful wool suit and knee socks to match her outfit. She walked with a stride, carrying shopping bags. Mae Etta and Robert ran to meet her while Christine tottered behind. The bags changed hands before the team entered the door.

The brother and sisters gathered around the girl who had been away for just a few months that seemed like a long time. They laughed and greeted each other with their eyes glued to the bags.

Amma and I observed from a distance, and I could feel the smile on my face.

We came out of our trance when I heard Ida Lee say, "We're gonna open our presents on Christmas morning."

"Oh, no!" Mae Etta exclaimed.

Still excited about the arrival of his sister, Robert jumped up and down as he said, "I can't wait 'til Christmas day to open mine!"

Ida Lee wanted to know if Buddy would be home for Christmas.

Amma was the first one to speak, "We talked 'bout that, but we have no way of knowing. Ted should know that we wanta' see him at Christmas time."

With that being said, she left the room. I guess she didn't want the children to see her sadness or maybe tears. I could hear dishes rattling. When I entered the kitchen, she was scurrying about getting dinner ready.

For dinner, we had string beans from our garden. Our canned vegetables were still adequate for the winter. The meat of the non-laying hen was in the skillet. I could smell the aroma of the biscuits from the oven.

We spent most of our dinnertime catching up on things that happened while Ida Lee was away. In the middle of the conversation, my daughter said, "I met a nice man on the bus coming home."

I didn't speak. In fact, I couldn't speak. I just bowed my head, continuing to eat. I couldn't get excited about this man until I was sure he was someone that was worthy of my daughter. Once I got to know him and found that he was deserving of her, I would give them my blessings. In the meantime, I would wait to see what the future had in store.

On the other hand, Amma seemed anxious to hear about him. With glowing eyes and a smile piercing her lips, she asked, "Whata 'bout this young man you met?"

Ida Lee went on to say, "When he got on the bus, he sat beside me. I found out that we were from the same hometown. He grew up in the city and attended West Side High School. Then, he went off to the service after finishing school. Just the way most of the boys did 'round here."

With excitement in her voice, Mae Etta asked, "What does he look like?"

"He's a good-looking sailor, and seems to be a real gentleman," Ida Lee said, as her eyes sparkled with happiness. "You'll see him."

"When will we see him?" Mae Etta asked, with excitement on her face.

Sounding hopeful, my oldest daughter stated, "He said he was coming on Christmas day."

Mae Etta didn't seem to believe that the young man had mustered the courage to come to our house a few days after meeting Ida Lee on the bus. With wide eyes, she asked, "Really? He's coming . . . here . . . to our house . . . on Christmas day?"

Ida Lee's face suddenly became somber, and she spouted, "Yeah! Why not?"

The conversation was not one of my interest, so my mind wandered to my duties outside. There was always something I could do. The weather was getting cold, and I could gather firewood for the winter. Tree trunks were waiting for me to split. My mind wandered on and on. I think Ida Lee observed my nonchalant expression and switched the subject. She began to tell us about her friend, Anna Jones.

Anna's parents had afforded her the opportunity to attend high school at Palmer Memorial Institute. She was spending time with her aunt in Greensboro and would be home for the summer. I was more excited when I heard Ida Lee say that she and Anna would be back home for the summer.

Long after dinner, Amma and the children sat at the kitchen

table, talking about any and everything while I carried in wood, putting it in the box behind the stove.

Before I could leave the kitchen, Amma asked, "Joey, you remember old man Jackson who lives in Prim Brook?"

"Yeah, I do. Haven't seen him for a long time. Whata 'bout him?" I asked, as I stood by the door to exit.

A small smile crossed Amma's face as she announced, "That was his grandson that Ida Lee met on the bus."

"Whata you know? Jackson's still there in Prim Brook? I wonder if he's staying by himself," I said, with a distinct picture of the little old man with no teeth.

Ada Lee said, "Yes, he is staying by himself. Jasper was anxious to get home to see him."

With that being said, I left the hen-talking to the women.

~~~~~~~~~~

Christmas Eve came, while the ladies spend the whole day cooking and chatting. Laughter fluttered around the kitchen. The chocolate, walnut, and coconut cakes were piled high enough to tumble over. From the outside, I spied apple and potato pies cooling on the window ledges. I guessed that the aroma was trailing from our house, hanging low, and permeating the neighborhood.

A chill was in the air, and we even had a few flakes of snow, but not enough for Amma to make snow cream. Who cared about the snow? Let it snow. It was Christmas time and my daughter, Miss Santa Claus, had come to town with Christmas cheers and gifts.

When night fell, Robert and Christine were in bed, as usual. I nodded off in my usual comfortable chair, and Amma did her reading, praying, and humming. Ida Lee and Mae Etta talked and giggled late into the night.

Before the light of daybreak could hit the hooks on the curtains, Mae Etta and Robert clamored from their beds and soldierly sat staring at the gifts under the Christmas tree.

Before long, the whole household was up, even little Christine. The resourceful Ida Lee, respectfully, handed out gifts. She handed Amma a box that was nestled in red Christmas paper with a big bright bow on top. All eyes were on her as she genteelly opened her present. Her face lit up like a Christmas tree when she peeked inside the box. She then gave us a generous smile while pulling the pink, soft, flowing nightgown from its wrappings, and swooped it around her. The sight of her chilled me.

An "*e-eek*" came from little Christine's mouth when she caught sight of her soft, brown doll with black, curly hair. Suddenly, our eyes were fixed on the beautiful doll. Obviously, we had never set eyes on a colored doll. Some of the family reached out to touch her, but I sat stoic, resembling a soldier. Christine tightly hung on to that baby doll, sweetly kissing her dimples. Our words became a siren song, "*O-o-oh, how sweet! A colored doll!*"

Blessings had just walked right into our front door and were shining on us on Christmas morning. Ida Lee handed me a box that had a shimming gold wrapping. For a while, I eyed the bow that resembled a necktie. When I gathered the courage to break through the handsomeness, I was in awe. I never dreamed of having a pair of work socks for every day of the week. Why, Amma had patched my old socks a thousand times, and still they were as holey as Swiss cheese! Everyone had their eyes on me as if I was supposed to make a speech. Searching my mind and soul, I uttered, "Bless the Lord! How Great Thou are!"

Amma followed up with, "Thank You, Lawd! Thank You, Jesus!"

Long after breakfast, we still sat around the table. I was sipping coffee and listening to the radio. Robert was on the floor playing with his Christmas present. With vigor and vitality, he engineered his toy train around and around the imaginary tracks. Robert had great imagination and gave voice to his play.

Mae Etta pranced around the house in her new red sweater. Red was her favorite color. I heard Ida Lee teasing her about saving up money for years to buy a pair of red shoes.

Buddy's gift was alone under the Christmas tree until late in the morning. I suppose someone had put it away when I again peeked in the living room.

Amma and the girls had spent hours in the kitchen, and I could guess that the Christmas Day dinner was coming up soon. Leaving Robert and Christine at play, I put in a visit to the kitchen.

I noticed that Mae Etta's decorative jar of holly berry sprigs had been moved off the kitchen table to make enough room for our food. On the table, I spied the smoked, mouthwatering ham that I deliberately wrung out of Sam. Once in my possession, I hung it in my smokehouse until Christmas Eve. Without the hickory-smoked ham, we would have had to slaughter a laying hen. That would have cost us dearly. We were in need of all the eggs we could get.

Beside the ham, a bowl of frost-sweetened collard greens graced our table. Our earthly sweet potatoes lay ready for the spices. The potato salad was definitely potatoes, with missing ingredients from the recipe. Our cornbread was made from Amma's great-great-grandmother's recipe, which called for the bare necessities, but tasted like a million dollars. The golden-brown bread was served in triangles, straight from a cast-iron pan.

On the back of the stove was a simmering pot of pinto beans, which had become a very special dish, close to our hearts. They were a big hit with all the members of the family. We had a wealth of dried beans and peas in our household, and they were simple to cook on our wood-burning stove, plus, they were filling.

Deciding what to cook and put on our table was not a challenge. We joyfully pulled together what we had, and we had a plenty. We then gathered around the table, mindful of our one absent child. With bowed heads, we humbly thanked God for His blessings, while asking Him to remember Buddy.

When Amma finished her long prayer, we delighted in the

main course of our meal. After polishing off the staple foods, we then eyed the deserts.

Our trees gave us walnuts and pecans, so naturally, everyone looked forward to Amma's towering walnut cake. The chocolate cake, topped with pecans, was also a big hit.

Meanwhile, Ida Lee had begun to slice her favorite, one of the delectable sweet potato pies, while Mae Etta went for the apple pie. Amma rolled her own dough with a wooden rolling pin, and hand-grated her coconut. Like those family ladies who went before her, she would painstakingly design her pie crust.

Late in the afternoon, the sun peeked from behind the clouds. With the realization that the night chill would demand a fire in the heater, I went after a log with a vengeance until a truck with two young men rolled up in front of the house. A soldierly looking man got out, went to the front door, and someone let him inside. Though, I didn't know for certain, I strongly suspected that he was the guy Ida Lee had met on the bus.

When I entered the house, I noticed that everyone seemed very excited, except for me, of course. I was, well, the father of the beautiful girl. The guy stood in the middle of the room, as the children stood around him, listening hard and thoroughly, and seemingly, enjoying every moment. Robert had left his toy train behind and was standing barefooted. Christine stood, still holding on to her lovely brown doll, as she gazed up at the tall man. Amma had gotten lost in the kitchen, and Mae Etta stayed aloof, of course.

Disregarding the others, the young man quickly turned to me and said, "I'm Jasper Jackson, Mr. Randall Jackson's grandson."

"Who's your father?" I asked, and then thought, "What a ridiculous question." So, I quickly said, "Oh, I do know Mr. Jackson, who lives over in Prim Brook."

"I thought you would know him," Jasper said, as he looked into my daughter's beautiful brown eyes, ignoring me as he said to her, "My grandfather will love you."

Swallowing hard and clearing my throat, I stuttered, "Mr. Jackson - he – he's - a fine man." At the same time, I was backing up and stepping back out the door, where I started breathing again.

The young man stayed a short time and was unable to talk to Ida Lee alone. Later, Amma did mention to me that on the way out the door, Jasper promised to see Ida Lee again. She then described the scene when the young man was leaving. She said that Ida Lee stood at the door to see him off, while Mae Etta pulled the curtains back and peeked through the window to get a better glimpse, and Robert and Christine ran off to play with their Christmas toys.

2 CHAPTER TWO

MAE ETTA

"Success is to be measured

not so much by the position

that one has reached in life

as by the obstacles which he has overcome."

~ Booker T. Washington

The year of 1957 came in with a big bang. In my head, the hot glowing sparks flew and scattered all over the place. I was about to graduate from high school and had the second highest ranking in my graduating class. Mrs. Rouse, my English teacher, seemed to be as excited as I was when we were preparing the salutatory address to be delivered at the commencement exercise. My dreams soared to great height, higher than the trees . . . the mountains . . . the skies!

I made a dramatic attempt to explain to my parents, about my partial scholarship to St. Augustine College in Raleigh, North Carolina. After searching for words and rearranging my sentences, I realized that discussing my going off to college with mama was synonymous to trying to tell her about my desire to go to the moon. No matter how much I tried to get through, mama's brain could not conceive of my going to college.

Our discussion seemed like what it must be like to try and

build a space ship! She asked questions that only a space biologist could answer. For weeks, mama and I built a spaceship in our conversation. We went far beyond the atmosphere of the earth. Mama just couldn't get the idea that college was a place here on earth. When I found that there was no coming down to ground level, I decided to drop the matter altogether.

Seemingly, my going to college was becoming a wild fancy, a hope-------a desire-----or maybe, just a dream. As the days went by, I felt like a numbskull, I cried at the drop of a hat. I am sure it showed in my school work and talks with Mrs. Rouse. Discussing my problem with my teacher was out of the question. As a rule, we let family business stay within our household and under our roof.

At the black schools in Craven County, we didn't have hired secretaries in the principal's offices. The upper high school students worked the office, answering the telephone, taking messages, etc. I was one of the young ladies that landed one of these non-paying jobs. One day, Mrs. Pugh, a black lady, who was the supervisor for the Craven County Black Schools, came into the office. While waiting for the principal, she asked about my plans after high school.

Looking in the opposite direction, I tried to think of a good lie, but we were taught that it was a sin to tell a lie. So, I blurted out everything about my trying to get my parents to understand that there was a way for me to go to college. I knew that I was the first in the family, and most of the relatives thought that going to college was not in the picture. Tears flowed as I said, "This is my dream! I don't know anything else I want to do!"

Mrs. Pugh asked, "Do you think I should talk to your parents?"

"No! No!" I cried, as tears flowed down my face.

The lady sat in deep thought, and looked into the yonder as she uttered, "Uh-h-h-h, let's pray."

Mrs. Pugh's beautiful prayers heightened the level of my senses. She said all the things that I would have said to the Lord. Her words deliberately rolled of her tongue, and they were so distinct that I knew the Heavenly Father understood. I was not ready for her to say, "Amen," but she did. She raised her head, gave me a pat on the back and a wink of the eye, and walked gracefully into the principal's cubbyhole of an office. That holy prayer, gentle pat, and precious wink, cleared my head of all my worries. I didn't know what I was going to say to mama, but I realized with certainty that I was going to college one day.

Over the next few days, mama and I talked about taking a trip to the college that had awarded me the scholarship for two hundred dollars. Mama always tried to comply with our wishes if she felt that they were beneficial. For some reason, she could see the need for the visit. We had no telephone; so, as always, mama wrote a letter to Uncle Roy, asking if he could take us to St. Augustine College in Raleigh, North Carolina.

Uncle Roy would never reply to our letters. Most of the time, he would come on the date that was planned. If he was unable to come, he would try to come by to inform us that he could not come on said date. When he failed to inform us, we painfully waited, sometimes, in vain. If there was a no-show, the younger ones had trouble brushing the trip off, and lived in agony for the next few hours, or maybe, the rest of the day. However, mama and daddy had the mind and spirit to face just about anything. They readjusted and cheerfully went about the day if he did not show.

However, for our college trip, in early March, Uncle Roy did show. On that particular spring morning, when he arrived, I was so happy, and could not wait in the house. I skipped out into the yard and tiptoed through the kaleidoscope of bold colored tulips. I winked at the azaleas that were putting on a show. I skipped all the way to the car, said my---- "Good Morning", to Uncle Roy, as I jumped in the back seat with my cousin, who was going along for the ride.

We were on our way to a college, a place that we had never been. As we left the house, mama stood stone faced by the highway, and seemed to be deep in thought. Christine held her brown doll and Robert stood beside her, waving their little hands, and looking happy, as always.

The driver, Uncle Roy, was one of mama's brothers. Of course, there were ten of them. This one was another farmer, and a hard worker who embraced optimism enough to drive us to the campus. It was said that he was very level-headed and was doing quite well financially, but strongly suspected to have hit the glass ceiling. We were all aware that the bar for a black man was set very low, and if a black was determined, he will rise above the expected level, and break through the ceiling.

On the right of my Uncle Roy, daddy boldly sat, looking straight ahead with his high cheekbones and beautiful brown eyes. Just maybe, he was wondering what the future had in store for all of us, especially me. Before this day, the discussion was held with mama, and if she would make the plan, daddy usually would go along with the program. On this day, he seemed very comfortable, showing no signs of fearful anticipations.

I huddled in the spacious back seat of my uncle's Chevy, looking out the window. The view was fascinating, and I could barely pull my eyes away from the scene outside.

My cousin, who sat on the right of me, had probably never been out of Craven County, much less to a college campus. Pressing close against the side of the car, leaving a healthy space between us, he continuously licked the brown froth on his lips. Every so often, he poked his head out the window and spat. A long stream of tobacco juice flew in the wind. He then wiped his mouth with his already smeared sleeves, alternating the right and left.

For the most part, silence permeated the car as we made the journey to St. Augustine College. In the stillness of the Chevy, I could hear the disquieting voice of my daddy echoing in my ears:

"You must get a good education to help change this unequal society, but it won't be easy. You must have your wits about you at all times and be willing to press forward no matter what happens. Carry a big stick with persistence and determination."

Joey Bloomfield was somewhat a fan of Booker T. Washington and felt that the man was one of the most influential black leaders in American in his time. As if Booker T. were a buddy of his, with whom he had much association, he would say, "I feel partly like Booker T. He believed that the best interests of blacks would be gained through education and economic status."   Many Black leaders disagreed with Booker T. Washington. They thought that he pleased many whites in order to gain financial support for Tuskegee Institute in Alabama, a school for blacks that stressed vocational training.

Daddy was inclined to lean toward the great Booker T. Washington; however, he felt that maybe the leader had put the cart before the horse. He found it impressive that Booker T. did get financial support for Tuskegee Institute in Alabama and believed that the vocational training school was greatly needed for the black race.

As I studied the great civil rights leaders, it became clear --- they all agreed that something should be done about the "Jim Crow" laws; but, like anything else, they disagreed on what exactly should be done and how to go about it.

The ride to Raleigh reminded me of the rugged journey to Montgomery, Alabama of which my father so often spoke. In the depths of my heart, I felt that I was on a freedom ride, searching for hope. I knew that much, that fighting for freedom was a condition of the world, and the fight was "ON" for my generation and generations to come.

~~~~~~~~~~

Around noonday, when the sun had hit its apex, we rode onto campus, and parked under a big shady tree. The sprawling limbs spread over the car like an umbrella. With a dramatic flair, I sprung out of the car and walked with a stride ahead of the others, as daddy gave me a go-ahead-look. The sun shined warmly, and my eyes burned from the harshness of the wind that had beat on my face through the open car window.

Simmering in the back of my mind was what my English teacher, Mrs. Rouse, and I had discussed. She had informed me to first find the Administration Building where I would probably get assistance.

"Don't be shy; and, speak up for goodness sake," she had admonished me.

Inside the building, the halls were full of pictures and written history of the school. St. Augustine was founded in 1867 for the education of freed slaves. The school was located about 10 blocks east of the capital in Raleigh, North Carolina. The black college was started under the auspices of a religious organization, the Episcopal Church. In 1954, the Supreme Court ruled in "Brown v. Board of Education of Topeka, Kansas" that segregation in the public schools was "unconstitutional", but my father declared that it would be decades before Jim Crow would begin to unravel. Many white people didn't think Negroes had souls. They thought we were just animals. Undoing the mess that was created would take some time.

As I glanced at the picture of Henry Beard Delany, I drifted away in deep thought: Mrs. Rouse had attended St. Augustine, and had been a friend of the feisty Bessie Delany, while she spent time with the family in their cottage on campus. She wanted me to attend the college, and had said I was more like Sweet Sadie Delany, with the same quiet determination. My English teacher familiarized me with the family, saying that Henry was born in slavery, yet, became the nation's first elected black Episcopal bishop, and was later vice-principal at St. Augustine School. His wife, Nanny, could have passed for white, but chose not to. Nanny Logan Delany buttressed her principal husband's career by working as the school's matron, actively supporting his child-rearing efforts. While at the school, she had taught Mrs. Rouse cooking.

Taking a look at daddy, I could tell that he maintained bright prospects for my future. He joined me with excitement when we noticed a picture of Mr. Delany and Mr. Du Bois in the hallway. They were sitting together, and the script below the frame explained that they were discussing "The Jim Crow Laws."

Daddy denied that he had the ability to read, but he sure had a lot of information in that round head of his. He would tell us about the Jim Crow Laws that were designed to discriminate against and suppress black people. He explained, "The Laws became entrenched in Southern society in 1896, when the Supreme Court ruled in the *Plessy v. Ferguson* case. The case stemmed from an incident in which a Louisiana shoemaker named Homer Aldolph Plessy refused to leave the "white only" railroad car on June 7, 1892. He lost his appeal to the Supreme Court, which sanctioned the establishment of the "separate but equal" doctrine for blacks and whites. The laws forcibly segregated blacks in communities, schools, hospitals, restaurants, prisons, the military, and cemeteries. The restrictions applied to public rest rooms, water fountains, public transportation, and employment."

We had talked about W.E.B. Du Bois in our history class and learned that he helped launch the National Association for the Advancement of Colored People (N.A.A.C.P.) in 1909, demanding that African-Americans achieve economic equality as well as full and immediate civil and political equality.

Mama and daddy were members of the N.A.A.C.P., while membership dues were paid by a benefactor.

When we ended up in the admissions office, all went well until we were told what the private college would cost per year. I had been honored with a two-hundred-dollars scholarship from my high school, Newbold Training High, but the tuition for the year at St. Augustine was eight-hundred-dollars. Mr. Manning, the administrator, graciously talked about a work study program; but, I think the large sum of money that we couldn't comprehend numbed us. Daddy's face was stern as he looked straight ahead.

My daddy's silence affected me. I went deaf for a while and was frozen in my seat, but later managed to glance at daddy, who had managed to put a smile on his face. Quietness continued to mingle around us, and when my mind had thawed somewhat, I remembered Mrs. Rouse's instructions on how to end the visit. I quickly and quietly said, "Thanks so much for spending time with us. We will get back with you." Then we stood and shook hands, as Mr. Manning smiled with seemingly complete satisfaction and thanked us for choosing St. Augustine, promising that more paperwork would be arriving in the mail.

We walked soldierly out of the building and made our way to the waiting car. My uncle and cousin had chosen to roam around the campus while we took care of business. Daddy and I stood under the shade tree, while silence hung in the air. I felt embarrassed about suggesting such a trip. After all, my parents were penniless most of the time. Never-the-less, they provided for us through hard work; however, I had no desire to extend their exile of punishment. It seemed that the whole world had come to a halt, and I truly wanted to get off. I suddenly realized that I must have been driven by hunger for success to make such a suggestion.

Quietness permeated the inside of the Chevy as we rode back to our house in Jasper. The sun stayed behind the clouds and sank early in the day. That figure----*eight-hundred-dollars*--- hammered away in my head until I developed a pounding headache. I knew that some way I had to keep myself in a grip of sanity. I said aloud, "Where there is a will, there is a way." Eyes widened, and ears strained, but silence persisted as we rode toward our happy home.

"The Lord didn't intend for His people to be worried," Mama would always say. So, I tried not to worry about how I would get to college; instead, buried myself in my school books while writing my salutatory speech.

~~~~~~~~~~

The winter weather had abated, and spring had sprung. Mama had found little time to spend on her precious spot of soil . . . her flower garden. Thus, while we visited St. Augustine College, she went into an inventive mood with her own unique approach. The tulips, daffodils and lilies had already said their "welcome to spring." They were so reliable; they multiplied every year, and they needed thinning. After digging up some of them, my mother would set them across the road where they continued growing, which other flower lovers welcomed.

Being a crafty and innovative gardener, mama gave soil care to her azaleas, camellias, gardenias, hydrangeas, and the like. She had no fear of trying something new in her garden. If a plant didn't survive the first time around, she would try again and again. She was not afraid to go out in the garden, get on her knees, play in the soil, and get her hands dirty.

We all looked forward to the plant of spring . . . the gorgeous purple Japanese Kerrie, which grew near the chicken fence.

Mama made sure that her summer plants were planted early enough to grow good root systems before the weather got too hot. She was fond of roses, but also loved her marigolds, impatiens, zinnias, begonias, and some she couldn't name. When she visited someone who had a plant she didn't have, she would politely ask for a shoot. On the other hand, people stopped by our place and gathered pieces of plants or even bouquets.

The most challenging thing about our garden was the height of the plants. The taller ones should have had their place, so that the smaller ones could be seen. Of course, Mama just found a spot when he received a new shoot.

The walkway to our house was always accented with verbenas, dianthus, and the like.

Rounded clusters of dianthus, sweeping petunias, and other brightly colored flowers decorated our freestanding buckets on the sides of the steps.

In our haven, a gigantic crepe myrtle with its gorgeous

flowers, stood with spreading limbs in our front yard. That was our place for taking black and white pictures with our one and only camera, and it was also a beautiful, shady spot to enjoy with friends. Sometimes, we even used the spot for lovers' lane . . . that is, if we thought mama wasn't around. Kissing with our boyfriends was a private thing, but sometimes we did get caught.

Ida Lee had the same boyfriend throughout most of high school, but, Anna and I changed boyfriends like we changed shoes, and we each had a so-called boyfriend since the first grade. As a group, we loved to attend the drive-in movie theater on Friday or Saturday nights. We found that the drive-in was so ideal for dating.

Our group of friends loved the fascination of the large, outdoor screen, and the good tasting pop-corn from the concession stand. The idea of viewing the movies on a big screen, from the comfort of our car, with the hanging window speaker attached by a wire, seemed romantic.

We had to be home soon after the movie ended. Of course, mama knew what time the show was over. If we broke the rule, we had to pay the price. There was no come to Jesus meeting, or apologies. Our punishment was written in stone . . . sealed, bonded, and carried out to a tee.

Mama had her saintly, quiet way of spelling out the details of the punishment, "You'll be staying out of school for the next two Wednesdays and doin' the washing."

Doing the laundry wasn't as much the problem as staying out of school. We were deeply rooted in school, and we loved every second there. Our minds and souls were torn apart if we had to miss a day. School supplied our physical, social, and psychological well-being.

3 CHAPTER THREE

JOEY

"I don't feel obligated to believe

that the same God who has endowed us

with sense, reason and intellect

has intended us to forgo their use.

~ Galileo Galilei

Late in March, I was working at odd jobs, but took time for plowing my garden, turning over the soil, and burying the fall leaves, stalks, roots, and weeds. As I rushed behind the mule that I had borrowed, I gazed at Sadie's part of the property that was overgrown with weeds, dandelions, and briars. I had a mind to turn over the soil on her portion of land, but my wounded feelings overpowered my actions. For years, our property had been the center of our fights.

Just as I was about to collect my thoughts, I caught sight of smoke propelling from Sadie's house. Quickly tying the mule to an apple tree, I rushed toward the old weather-beaten plank house just as Sadie ran out on to the porch yelling, "My house is on fire!" Her words became a siren song. Her small frame threw the two rockers off the porch, and then took a dive with clothing hanging from her like Spanish moss on a tree. Only the whites of her eyes showed, and her face seemed different in contrast to what it once was. She stiffened at the sight of me.

I could not allow myself to soothe her with words; but, I instantly turned around and ran for water from our pump. Amma joined me in the struggle. We quickened our steps, but the uncontrollable fire rose higher. Feeling that I could not contain the fire, I sped toward Jasper on my bike to get to a telephone and call the Jasper fire department. The wind was at my back, and the fresh air smelled better than the roasting house.

Out of nowhere, I heard the beeping of a fire engine; and then, I saw the red truck go by me. I placed my hand over my ears to deafen the loud squeaking sound. In the distance, behind me, the engine's whistle faded, and then, it disappeared from sight. I was relieved to know that someone had sent the fire engine to the burning plank house. As if I couldn't change directions, I looked straight ahead, and pedaled on and on, until I found myself in front of my friend, Berman's house.

Jumping off my bike and putting the stand down, I ran to my friend's front door. When I began knocking, the door flew open. Berman stared at me as I tried to tell him the news. Then, I let out the breath that I had been holding and was able to say, "Sadie's house is on fire."

With haste, my bike was tied in the trunk of the car. We quickly jumped inside the cab and made our way back down the road toward the disaster. Arriving at Sadie's place, we noticed that the flames were gone, and the dusty smoke floated above. The watering hose that the two firemen held in their hands had done the job.

The firemen spoke to us, but Berman and I knew very little. Sadie was scared stupid. She walked around in a circle until seemingly her knees gave out, and she then eased down on the ground and didn't seem to be capable of drawing her next breath.

The men from the fire house showed great concern for the lady, and even I had a slither of uneasiness way down my spine. We helped her onto her feet, and a faint smile flickered upon her face. She said, "I'm alright," and then walked toward the smoldering house. We could hear the squishy, squashy noises in her shoes. The sound told the story of the many buckets of water the woman had handled.

The three of us watched the red tail of the truck disappear into the distance of the bright sunlight. The two firemen had done their work and were on their way back to the station, leaving us alone.

Having nothing else imaginable to do, Berman and I walked over to the upheaved chairs and put them in an upright position. Sadie sat in a chair while she retrieved her items from the ground—the few things she had desperately saved from the fiery building. In her hand, she held a black jacket that had been on a hook by the front door. "My Mom's old jacket!" She proudly announced.

We stood looking at Sadie in amazement. Then, Berman got my attention and insisted that I sit in the other chair, as he lowered himself to the ground.

At that moment, we were all probably thinking about the same thing—where Sadie was going to stay. I looked over at the lady and saw that tears had made white streaks on her smooth, black skin. She commented, "I dun' lost all that'a had." She then lifted the tail of her dress and wiped her face.

I tried to remain calm and show respect, but the tragedy had happened to *our* home place no matter how much Sadie had insisted on it being hers. I then said, "I'm sorry, Sadie. Really, I am. Sorry, for us all."

Instead of answering, she grimaced. I could tell that she was trying to maintain her composure. Her voice came out soft as she rubbed her hands together and gripped the arms of her chair, and said, "I wonder why we never gotta' long?"

I took a deep breath as I wanted to say, *"Fool, you are the old lady who keeps up the fuss."*

When Berman noticed our fierce expressions, he walked away, way behind the smoldering house.

When he seemed to be out of hearing distance, I stood up,

and said pointedly, "My mom died when I was a baby. You became one of those dadgum grown-ups that was 'pose to be helping me. But seems like you never wanted me to stay here on my grand-daddy's land. I pay all the tax, and you still ain't satisfied."

"Yeah. I'm one of the grown-ups that took good care of you. You sho' should be nice to me, boy," Sadie said, trying to let the hard, grim line of her mouth go to soft, sweet curves . . . none of which she ever possessed.

Remembering how she had cursed at my wife, Amma, I answered, "You should be nicer to us."

"Who's we talking 'bout here, you or her?" Sadie asked.

"You know dadgum well who I am talking 'bout. Me and my wife . . . us," I said to her, for the umpteenth time.

"Hell, I'm talking to you, just you. She ain't out here," She stated, sounding genuinely angry.

"Drop it," I said.

The woman who was supposed to be my loving aunt grunted and cursed as she always did, when she could think of nothing else to say.

After standing his distance, Berman appeared with a suggestion, "Sadie, you want to go to yo' brother's house to see if you can spend the night?"

"Reckon I will," Sadie said, looking straight at me.

"You sho' should go someplace, if you know what I mean," I stated.

"I'm not stupid, I won't be coming to yo' house," she said, with a throbbing sound from the base of her throat that showed how frustrated she really was.

I said, "No way in hell would you stay with Amma and me."

Sadie casted her red eyes at me and twisted her mouth in her usual cursing formation, as Berman ushered her to his car.

For years, Berman had been one of the go-betweens . . . for Sadie and me. He knew all about our property struggle. He desperately wanted us to get along. I felt that he and Amma were condescendingly courteous. The two of them seemed to respond to Sadie's insults with gracious humor. On the other hand, Berman and Amma had completely different approaches in the compassion each showed the older lady. While my friend tried to keep everyone calm with gracious words, my wife wore the scriptures from the Bible on her sleeves and spoke them whenever she saw fit.

Not me! When someone said something to invoke evil on me or my family, I had enough in my vocabulary to give back; and, I would let go!!! Curtailing my vocabulary, if Amma or the children were present.

~~~~~~~~~~

The burning smell was in my nose, and my eyes teared as I started next door to my house, but then I remembered the mule that had been tied to the tree for hours. I felt terrible for forgetting about the animal, but when I reached him, he seemed happy, and didn't seem as flustered as I was. He had munched on all the vegetation that was within reach. In fact, he was still crunching as I untied him, and in my own way, I tried to beg his forgiveness. Being well aware that our apple tree would not bear very much fruit this year, I was sorry that I had to use the tree as a hitching post.

The furry animal had been granted a furlough for the day and was ready to be hitched to the wagon to return to his home. I sat behind the mule, and there ahead of us, among the treetops, the sunset blazed with all its glory. There was a smell of horse manure in the breeze. I imagined that the soil would be highly productive during the growing season.

When the mule had been put away, I masterly told Dave, the owner, all about the day before returning home.

Dave said a few comforting words to me, as he was aware of the property misunderstanding and my Aunt Sadie's selfish maneuvers.

At home, I opened the door as Amma greeted me with a

questionable look. I could tell that she wanted to know if Sadie and I had argued.

"How is Sadie taking things?" Amma asked.

"She is desperate, but she didn't exactly fall apart," I announced.

Amma bubbled over with questions, "I can't imagine Sadie weeping, but was she weeping? Was she cussing and swearing? Where's she now? Who is gonna keep her?"

I let Amma get a few questions off her brain before I held my hand up for her to stop and take a breath. When she stopped, I said, "I know it seems impossible for Sadie to weep, 'cause she is a hard knot and stronger than some females, but she was confused and frightened, and she did cuss."

"Did you cuss back at her?" Amma asked, realizing how much she had asked me not to return that kind of language.

"Naw, I just said, dadgum, and that ain't cussing, but I did tell her a few other things."

"What things?" Amma asked.

"That she wasn't gonna stay at my house," I said, as I drew my brows together and gritted my teeth, "but, I did say I was sorry about her losing everything . . . and I'm sho' glad she went on up there to stay with her brother, Henry . . . cause . . . "

Amma cut in before I could finish, and stated, "No, she ain't staying in this here house."

Dinner was ready and waiting on the back of the stove. For dinner, we had pork chops, potatoes from our 'tata' bank, canned string beans from our garden, and of course, we had peach preserves. As we pulled our chairs up to the table, we couldn't help but discuss Sadie and her burnt down house. As a matter of fact, none of us could remain calm about something as horrifying as our home place being destroyed by fire.

After dinner, I went out to replenish the water pails for the night. It was almost spring time, but the wind blew stiffly, while the moon shone brightly on the debris next door. I dared not go over and take a look through the ashes. If Sadie got any suspicion that I was over on, what she called 'her property' sifting through her belongings, she would swear that I had stolen her jewels.

When I returned to the house, I realized that the day's developments had taken its toll on all of us. The dishes were all done, and Mae Etta was still working on her homework. Bedtime came early for most of us. Amma walked sedately into our bedroom, said her prayers, crawled into bed, and stared at the ceiling.

Soon afterward, I dressed for bed, clicked off the light, crawled into bed beside her, and stared up at the same spot. I should have fallen asleep quickly, but instead, my muscles were tight, and my mind was stuck on all the events of the day. My thoughts spun like blades on a fan, as I dwelled on the tension that had been twinning itself between Sadie and me, for what seemed like forever. She must have had me pigeonholed long before I was old enough to remember. After all, it was not my fault that my mother died at my birth.

How I'd tried to discuss my mother with Sadie. Seems that she just didn't want to talk about her, and she would just say, "She died of a heart attack." Just about all the deaths I knew about stemmed from "heart attacks." Amma said, that was a way some families distanced themselves from thoughts of the unpleasantness of an infectious virus or certain diseases running in the family.

I later opened my eyes. The room was silent, and slivers of moonlight slashed the bureau. I could tell that daybreak had not emerged, so I stretched and attempted to go back to sleep. Amma had awakened and was in the kitchen rattling the pot and pans. Gently rolling over, I heard our dogs barking. Someone came through the front gate, so I got out of bed and peeked through the blind to see who it might be. Sadie, who never had the audacity to let her shadow come through our gate, was now coming to our door.

There was a loud shout.

I opened the door and starred at the red-eyed woman, who was standing somewhat unsteadily. Her soft, black, woolly hair was disarranged and looked tangled. Her dress hung from her like moss on a tree, as she held the same black jacket that she picked off the ground yesterday. She said, "Y'all know I lost everything. Don't you?"

"Come on in, Sadie," I said, reluctantly.

Amma walked in from the kitchen, wiping her hand on her apron. She was obviously shocked. Her gaze bore into Sadie as she uttered, "Set-- right -- in -- this here -- chair, Sadie."

The woman spread the jacket on the back of the chair and began to sit, nearly missing the chair. She scuffled but held onto the sides with her scraggy fingers.

Amma stood in front of her with suspicious, narrowed eyes, spreading her fingers on her midriff as if to say, *"Whata' you want?"*

Apparently, Sadie was feeling tense. She closed her eyes, and seemingly, tried to breathe deeply. Just maybe, she was trying to relax the knot that must have been in her stomach.

When my wife came out of her transfixion, she moved across the room to her favorite rocking chair. She then picked up her Bible from the nearby table. Shoulders slightly hunched, she gazed straight at Sadie, while opening her Bible. When she spoke, her voice was reasonable. "Sadie, usually I begin and end each day with prayers and scriptures. Will you join in with me this morning?"

Sadie squinted at Amma, as she twisted her hands in her lap. A wistful smile flicked across her face, and then, it faded away. She grasped for words, and finally said, "You goin' read anyway, no matter what I say. So, go on read."

Amma offered a lazy smile and raised her eyebrows, then said, "I'm goin' to read the 91st Psalms." Without looking up from the page, Amma began with Psalm 91:1:

"He who dwells in the shelter of the Most High,
who abides in the shadow of the Almighty,
will say to the Lord, "My refuge and my fortress;
My God, in whom I trust."

"For he will deliver you from the snare of the fowler
and from the deadly pestilence;
he will cover you with his pinions,
and under his wings you will find refuge;
his faithfulness is a shield and buckler.
You will not fear the terror of night,
nor the arrow that flies by day,
nor the pestilence that stalks in darkness,
nor the destruction that wastes at noonday."

"A thousand may fall at your side,
ten thousand at your right hand;
but it will not come near you.
You will only look with your eyes
and see the recompense of the wicked.
Because you have made the Lord your refuge.
the Most High your habitation,
no evil shall befall you, no scourge come near your tent."

Sadie stayed seated, idly picking at her dress without looking up at Amma.

Amma stopped at the end of the 9th chapter and paused, before going on and finishing the chapter.

Sadie only raised her eyeballs when Amma leaned slightly forward and asked, "Sadie, did you have anything to eat today?"

Out of the corner of her mouth, Sadie said, "Maybe, I should have mentioned this before, but I didn't come here to eat."

I butted in and asked, "Would you like a cup of coffee?"

With shoulders tensed, she answered, "Yeah, and something else if you got it, and don't mind giving me some."

Amma moved from her rocker and went to get the coffee. From the kitchen, she hollered, "I have some ham in here for the children's breakfast. I can make you a ham sandwich, Sadie."

Sounding stronger than ever, Sadie spoke up. "Reckon I

will. I ain't had nothin' to eat today."

With Amma in the kitchen, there was a silence in the room, with each of us being careful not to offend the other. Sadie took a deep breath. I cleared my throat and then began cracking my knuckles of my left hand. I looked at the clock with great anticipation that she would leave as soon as she finished the food.

Amma entered the room with a ham sandwich and a cup of coffee. She moved her Bible from the small table and pulled the table over to Sadie, placing the food on it. Sadie said, "Much obliged," and gobbled down the sandwich in no time, and then flushed it down with the cup of coffee. She then made an effort to talk.

Seeing that just maybe she had not been drinking moonshine, and since it seemed like she was finally in a sober talking mood, I asked, "Where'd you go last night?"

"I went up to Henry's house, but I ain't gonna go back there," Sadie said, with a sniffle.

"Y'all not getting along?" I asked.

"Nope! He don't want me staying in his house," Sadie said.

"You two been thick as thieves," I said with a grin, remembering how they ditched me.

Sadie stole glances at me, as she said, "As far as he's concerned, ain't no thickness no mo'."

"Y'all sho' know how to dig up dag'gone dirt together and sling it in my face," I just couldn't help myself, but I was the one who kept going back to the past. However, she hadn't helped to improve present day.

Again, Sadie fell silent. Maybe she was thinking before she spoke, so that she could choose her words. She knew that Amma would not stand for her to curse in her house. I was wondering how long she was going to stay. I was about to ask her when she suddenly spoke, "You know, I don't have to listen to a-a-ll this crap!" She then moved from her chair and yanked the black jacket off the back, and biting off each word evenly, she announced, "I'm . . . gonna . . . go . . . home." She was jabbing her arms into her jacket in an attempt to find the sleeves.

I rose from my chair and waited patiently while she struggled. I didn't want her to fall—not in my house. After all, I would have been reluctant to help her up. She probably would have wanted to sue me for touching her.

As Sadie worked with her jacket, going around in circles, Amma came from the kitchen to assess the situation.

I went over, opened the door, stood there soldierly, and waited for the jacket juggling to come to an end.

When Sadie finally finished chasing her jacket sleeve, she stepped outside.

Amma and I stood in the open doorway.

I asked, "Where you goin'?"

Sadie said, "Home."

"Home where?" Amma asked, wary.

Sadie pointed her bony finger at the damaged house that had almost burned to the ground, and said, "Right over yonder, in them there chairs."

Looking puzzled, Amma stated, "Well, I guess, home is where we make it."

As Sadie pranced around outside, Amma stepped out and stood by her side and softly spoke, "Just let me add one more thing, Sadie. God is in control. He could be your comforter if you would let Him."

Sadie swallowed back the lump that must have rose in her throat but remained silent.

It was moments before anyone spoke. Amma asked, "Could I say a word of prayer?"

In the past, Sadie hadn't appreciated Amma's prayers, but this particular morning, she seemed ready to accept anything that would help her situation. Clasping her ashy hands together, she stood as straight as her posture would allow.

Amma bowed her head, closed one eye and prayed:

"My Dear God, who is rich in Mercy, have mercy on Sadie.

Help her to trust in you. Make a way for her and show her the way she should go. Thank You, Lord, for your steadfast love, which goes with us today and will endure forever. Forgive us for the wrong words that we say to each other and forgive us for the love we don't show. Grant us peace and comfort this morning, knowing that You love us and have given your own dear Son for us. If You have given us Jesus, You will surely, with Him, graciously help Sadie in this time of need, through Jesus Christ, our Lord. Amen."

I couldn't trust Sadie behind a pin, so I kept both eyes wide open. To my amazement, Sadie had bowed her head. Seemed that she was enjoying every little bit of attention we gave her. She appeared to be listening, while Amma prayed. I thought, *"Time will bring about a change."*

When Amma said "Amen," Sadie opened her eyes, folded her arms, and walked away in silence.

I cocked my brows and smiled as I looked at Amma. She smiled back. Each of us probably had the same thoughts.

We had no idea what Sadie had on her mind as she lowered her head, moved through our front gate, and turned toward what used to be her house. Entering her driveway, she stopped, stood still for a while gazing at the remains, and then, she slowly moved toward the chairs, flopping down in one of them.

A whiff of smoke was still in the air, and it was a bit chilly outside, but the sun was shining, and visually, it was going to be a beautiful day. Amma and I walked around in our yard and pulled the dew-soaked patches of flattened weeds, while we continued to observe Sadie. We noticed that she had stretched out in the two chairs and was resting.

~~~~~~~~~~

We returned to the inside of the house and closed the door behind us. With slumped shoulders, we stared at each other as we took a breath of fresh air. According to the clock in the kitchen, Sadie had been at our house for over an hour.

Mae Etta and Robert were up and were getting their breakfast. I could tell by their expressions that they were not certain what was happening.

We said, "Good morning," to the children, then rushed to the window, and pulled the curtain back to take a peek at Sadie. The woman had turned over from one side to the other, but she still lay in the chairs among the overgrown weeds and untended jungle of flowers.

Mae Etta and Robert had finished their breakfast and went out on the side of the highway to catch the school buses. One went to the high school, and the other attended the elementary school. Christine, our twenty-three –month-old, was still sleeping.

Amma and I sat down to eat. We were up way before daybreak, and our morning had been long and thoroughly tested. We discussed Sadie's surprise visit but were interrupted by loud talking from the front. We pushed back our chairs and got up instantly. Wiping our mouths with the back of our hands, we rushed to the front door. Sadie was out front, attempting to talk with the children. We didn't know exactly how long she had been there, but taking time with the children, or being courteous to them, was something she had not done over the years. I could tell that Mae Etta and Robert were uncomfortable and were keeping a healthy distance away from Sadie. They had learned not to trust her and were afraid of her. She had frightened them so many times before, while viciously prowling around in the vicinity.

Then, as I continued to observe, to my surprise, they were talking, while looking for the buses to appear.

A few minutes later, we saw a yellow bus coming, but when it got to our house, it went on by. That was the Jasper High School bus that transported white children to their school. However, our buses were not far behind. Robert got on his bus to go to the Pleasant Hill Elementary School. Later, Mae Etta's bus arrived, and she took her bus to the New Bold Training High School in Dover.

With droopy shoulders, Sadie gingerly moved back toward her house, and we returned to our food. When we finished our breakfast, we peeked out once more. Sadie had again taken a seat among the weeds, looking straight ahead. I guess she was just sitting there because she didn't know what to do. Sadie had many people in her world, and I was sure she would find one of them, or one of them would find her.

We went about our day's work. Late in the day, I noticed that Sadie had stood up, seemingly to stretch her back. Then a car stopped, and she got in as if she expected the person. They drove off on highway 55.

4 CHAPTER FOUR

MAE ETTA

"The informality of family life

is a blessed condition

that allows us to become our best

while looking our worst."

~ Marge Kennedy

Early in the morning, I woke up from my dream. I had been having lots of dreams. Most of my dreams were about going off to college, but this dream was about a woman . . . one that had caused trouble over the years. She was as unkind to us in the dream . . . as she had been in real life. As I listened, it seemed the lady was in our house.

I decided to lie in bed until I felt it was safe to get up. Then, I put one leg over the side of the bed, paused and listened. My feet touched the floor lightly as I tip-toed out of my bedroom, through the kitchen, and peeked into the front room. I froze from the sight of her. She was sitting in a chair in our house and was *not* stumbling drunk. Nor was she cursing, swearing, or throwing cunja powder. *"Is this for real? Is she in our house?"* I asked myself. *"Mama and Daddy would not let her in our house,"* I thought.

Walking stealthily back to my room, feeling very uneasy, I dressed, and gathered my books for school. Robert joined me for breakfast. Afterward, we quietly went out to the pump to brush our teeth. Neither said a word.

Robert and I walked to the roadside to meet the school bus. After standing there for a while, I heard someone clear her throat. Glancing up, I faced Aunt Sadie who was already upon us. She seemed skittish when she tried to talk to us behind our parent's back. At those times, she would try to disguise who she really was, while putting up a deceptive front. We were definitely afraid of her creepy disposition, and we would resist her shenanigans. Our parents had taught us to never eat anything that she offered, but to be polite and never sass the elderly. If the older person was repugnant in any way, we were to dismiss them in a gracious way, if possible.

I was seventeen—years-old, about to graduate from high school, and had hopes of going off to college. As I recollected, Aunt Sadie was certainly one of those people who had somewhat reduced our quality of living ever since I could remember.

We don't know what truly happened before we came upon this earth, but we had heard many tales about the past. Each person told it in his favor. Surely, there had to be a secret buried somewhere for a family to dislike one member so vehemently.

Years before I could remember, Aunt Sadie had denounced our mama. That caused us not to be fond of her from the beginning of our lives. Mama was our mother; and to us, she was a saintly woman, until whipping time, that is, of course.

Sadie would express her aversion in difference ways. On most, Saturday evenings, she would come in from town, a frazzled woman from the consumption of too much alcohol. In that condition, she took her customary position on the side of the house facing us. Using profane language, she would denounce the dogs, cats, chickens, and maybe the garden plants, all while, staring in our direction. We heard her loud and clear. We were well aware of the fact that she was cognizant of to whom she was delivering the message.

The woman next door was devoid of shame and would remove certain clothing if she were in the mood. Depending on her temperament, she sometimes displayed other antisocial behaviors.

Many times, Dad would put on a performance, calling her a "low-down deviant", "a devil out of hell", or he would tell her that she had the "devil to pay." Of course, over the years of frustration, other names were designated to her as well.

On the other hand, Mama would pick her chances, and choose her methods. Maybe, on a day when the sun was shining in the clear blue yonder, and Sadie was just moseying around and piddling away the day, Mama would clear her throat to get her attention. Mentioning the weather initiated an opening to a conversation. Over the period of time, there were multifarious ways Mama employed to try to encourage Sadie to discontinue her blasphemy, and show more respect for us, and, of course, God. Mama went on to say that even animals and maybe even the plants might not appreciate her actions.

At the same time, Mama asked us to ignore Sadie, and go about our merry ways, as if nothing was going on.

No matter what was said or done on Saturday evening, on Sunday morning, Sadie was dressed smartly and in her Sunday best, all ready for church. Sometimes, we would observe her walking down her steps and crossing the highway, going over to the Methodist church.

After church, she had many visitors. People would come and go with lots of loud talking and merrymaking.

~~~~~~~~~~

While Aunt Sadie stood with us on the side of the highway, she looked like a wreck. I stuttered and stepped backward when she gazed at us with her red, puffy eyes. I suddenly gained the courage to listen to what she had to say, as Robert and I stood our distance. She tried to make light conversation but scrambled her words. We listened carefully, saying nothing. She then took a deep breath and blew her nose heavily into her handkerchief from her pocket. Coming up for air, she said, "Mae Etta, you sho' look pretty."

Twirling around on the heels of my black patent leather shoes, I said,   "Thanks, I feel pretty." I was wearing a flared pink print dress, pink socks, and a matching ribbon that held my ponytail back from my bangs.

She looked at Robert and said, "Robert, you sho' growing. You in what grade now?"

Robert said, "In the third grade."

"Uh-uh-uh, don't time fly?" Sadie asked, shaking her head.

I wished that Aunt Sadie would leave, and I could tell that Robert felt the same way. I started fiddling with my books and obviously looking past her, as I glanced down the highway. Robert's attention centered on kicking a rock, that he had discovered near his feet.

Again, Aunt Sadie cleared her throat, but before she could say anything, the buses came into sight. The first one was the Jasper High School bus. Of course, the white student's bus didn't stop. Pleasant Hill Elementary was the next one, and when it came to a halt, Robert bounced up the steps. A few minutes later, I was happily seated on a yellow bus, heading to Newbold Training School.

Sitting in the forefront of the bus, I gazed out the window. My thoughts drifted off on Ida Lee, and the idea of her coming home for my graduation warmed the cockles of my heart. Her leaving home left me in a quandary. She was my best friend since the day I was born. As time went by, we had an unmistakable bond. Our powerful friendship led to our dressing alike and sharing thoughts that we never would share with anyone else. It was not uncommon to see our heads together, laughing at each other's jokes.

Of course, we had our crazy fights, but it only meant that we complemented each other in our differences. We both had our strong points, and sometimes it took us a while to recognize that fact.

When I brought myself back from my daydreaming, I became aware of the voices flying back and forth across the school bus. Just then, everyone stood, ready to exit the bus. We had reached our destination . . . Newbold Training School.

I stood, giving considerable attention to the creases in my dress. Our Mama had taught us to dress to make ourselves happy, and I took great care of my clothes. She bought our clothes from a consignment store, where we had great choices and got more bang for our few bucks. Although, I must admit, brand new things did excite me, and I was looking forward to more prosperous days ahead.

Ida Lee and I would get dressed in our bargain best and walked to church with Daddy. We frequented the Baptist Church. The highway was busy on Sunday mornings as people were going to their respective places of worship. While walking on the side of the road, we filed behind our Daddy. Our shiny patient leather shoes took a beating from the fine rocks, and the tall grass whipped our legs, but nothing could override our dominant good spirits.

After crossing over a bridge, we were in the churchyard, facing a gray, stone building, with a cross on top. Other church folks came from here and there, and we walked into the vestibule, one at a time. On the inside, we were welcomed by fashionably dressed people who carried big smiles on their faces. The church women wore high-heeled shoes and gorgeous hats that resembled our mother's hats.

Daddy and his two daughters preferred the front pews, as "back seat" loomed large with ugliness in our minds. In front of us, the choir graced the spot behind the pulpit. The choir comforted us with familiar spirituals that permitted us to sing along. The Deacons and Preachers sat in the pulpit, and later, from behind the podium, Reverend Simmons read the scriptures and gave us biblical words of encouragement for earthly living as well as for the hereafter. Deacon Dawson prayed a lengthy prayer that covered the aspects of the universe. From the pulpit podium, Reverend Smith preached a sermon that echoed to the outside. The people in the pews rose to their feet, waving their hands and repeating, "Amen."

At the end of the church service, we never knew what the weather would serve us. Be it sun, rain, wind, or sleet, we moved home like inflated balloons.

After church, we had a day of rest at home, where we could recover and recharge for the coming week. On most Sundays, we spent time together as a family. Mama cooked a heavy dinner; and afterwards, she and Daddy took a walk together down highway 55.

At home, while growing up, Ida Lee spent her time cooking and reading. When Mama and Daddy were not at home, she would try one of her exotic recipes. Sometimes the food would be edible, and other times, one of the dogs enjoyed the eats.

While I had a creative spirit, writing, painting, dancing, and the like, Ida Lee loved romance novels, and she had an exchange system with some of the girls at school. However, Mama was not in favor of such reading.

As younger children, we loved spending time outside, bicycle riding, jumping rope, and playing hopscotch, hide and seek, and the like. The outdoor activities were shared with our brother, Buddy. We, undoubtedly, had barrels of fun.

As teenagers, our responsibilities increased, and more was expected of us. Most times, Buddy did not execute what was expected of him. He was full of life and had unrealistic ideas and notions that sometimes created a scene at home or resulted in a suspension from school.

As Buddy got older, he became more meddlesome and the drama at our house increased. Daddy stood over him with a clenched fist, too many times. We held our breath and prayed a lot. Mama would put up a warning, but it would go unheeded. As a sister to a brother, I expressed my displeasure to him, but there was no improvement.

As time passed, Buddy was habitually seen somewhere other than school on school days.

Mama and Daddy scolded him, and he made promises.

Unfortunately, contrary to what he had promised, eventually, school became a thing of the past for my brother and awkward moments sneaked into our household, wherein, Daddy became breathless with rage.

Mama and Daddy must have had long, up-till midnight discussions. They took another path and began the day with open dialogue with their first-born son. Mama preached against dropping out of school, tried spiritual revival, and then, she threatened him with the toughest of love.

On the other hand, Daddy reminded his son that education was a prize that we won with blood, sweat, and tears, and that he was showing dishonor and disrespect for the work that we had done in the past. Of course, Daddy reopened his conversation about his trip to Montgomery, Alabama. He reiterated how he had met Dr. Martin Luther King, Jr. and told Buddy about all that he had learned. He stated that Dr. King would be disappointed if any young man dropped out of school.

As time went by, my parents were pushed to the wall; so, they made a desperate decision. They made arrangements for Buddy to work on our Uncle Ted's farm. Our uncle lived on the other side of the Neuse River, and we were aware that we would not see Buddy very often.

When he left, he took a part of my heart with him. He was greatly missed, and there were moments of loneliness, but after all, through our threshold crept a sense of peace. Even with the serenity surrounding us, I still remember the day that he left.

The day was a perfect sky- blue day. There was not a cloud in the sky. Buddy had packed, and we were all in wait when Uncle Ted drove up in his new, red truck. Obviously, he was happy to have a new hand for his farm. He pulled up just after 1 o'clock on a Saturday. For a moment, nobody moved. It was impossible to know how Buddy felt, but it was a time like no other for me.

Uncle Ted cut his engine off and stepped outside the truck.

Buddy dragged an old beat-up suitcase behind him. Uncle Ted opened the door. Buddy silently got in the truck and huddled to one side. Ted said a few words to Mama and Daddy, said his goodbyes as he walked around to the driver's side, and then, he got in and drove off.

We walked back into the house that was quiet . . . too quiet.

~~~~~~~~~~

My Mama said, "The Lord works in mysterious ways."

Yes, he did, when Ida Lee came home for my graduation, and brought upon the scene, her high school friend, Anna Jones. We felt that Anna was one of the luckiest girls in the world when she went off to high school at Palmer Institute in the fall of 1952. Years before, back in elementary school, we welcomed her visits, like the sunshine. The girl seemed to know it all, and when she told us stories about the birds and the bees, our senses would go into overdrive. I'd been watching farm animals breed and reproduce all my life, but it was good to hear about people, real boys and girls that I knew. Hearing such juicy news only confirmed what we already suspected about our schoolmates.

Dancing was another of Anna's specialties, and we learned many steps under her instruction. We moved in succession from boogie-woogie, to the cha-cha, to the camel walk, and on to bop, and on to the swing. Although my mother spoke of dancing as a sin, we welcomed our friend's instructions with open arms.

On Anna's return home in 1957, we did not 'shake a leg'. Those elementary days were over and done with. On that particular trip, the talk was all about Palmer Memorial Institute.

5 CHAPTER FIVE

ANNA JONES

"Love is friendship that has caught fire.

It is quiet understanding, mutual confidence,

sharing and forgiving.

It is loyalty through good and bad times.

It settles for less than perfection and

makes allowances for human weaknesses."

~ Ann Landers

We were identified as the middle class or uppity Negroes. Our sprawling ten-room Victorian house sat on a few acres of land, and we owned two vehicles, a car and my dad's, so-called "neighborhood" truck. Mom graduated from Elizabeth City Teacher's College and was one of the neighborhood's respected school teachers. She played the piano for our church, and joined a number of prestigious organizations such as, "The National Council of Negro Women" and "Delta Sigma Theta Sorority, Inc." The women in these organizations worked together on issues affecting black women, their families, and communities. I learned early in life about the founders of these women's organizations.

Mary McLeod Bethune was the founder of "The National Council of Negro Women." She loomed large in my estimation when I became aware of her many claims to fame. The greatest was the fact that she had an impact on getting black women into military officer roles in the Women's Army Corps during World War II.

My heart beat with a rhythm of joy when I learned that Bethune was a loyal friend of Eleanor and Franklin Roosevelt and was appointed to the position of Director of the Division of Negro Affairs, and as such, became the first female African - American federal agency head. She, in turn, was responsible for releasing National Youth Administration (NYA) funds to help black students through school-based programs. Bethune made sure black colleges participated in the "Civilian Pilot Training Program", which graduated some of the first black pilots. The NYA's final report was issued in 1943, and it stated that more than 300,000 black young men and women were given employment and work training as the result of the program. My mom, Mrs. Annabelle Jones, often spoke of Mary McLeod Bethune as a captain of a ship that brought many of us through a fog, and my mom said that it was up to us to continue the trip.

When I was quite young, I gained an interest in the Delta Sigma Theta Sorority. I learned that the sorority was a nonprofit organization that focused their efforts primarily on the black community, but they also provided assistance and support throughout the world. I knew of many girls who received college scholarships from the sorority. To me, it sounded like an extraordinary group, and I decided that one day I would join them.

~~~~~~~~~~

Dad was *Mr. Gilbert Jones,* who had earned a degree in construction from North Carolina Agricultural Technical College (A&T) and served his community well. I could hear the truck start up at any and all times of the night, as dad rushed to the aid of someone who needed a ride here, or there. When it came to the weather, he was always optimistic, and would let nothing slow him down. Many times, I heard him say, "God gave us life, health, food, and shelter; and, he gave those things to us for a reason."

Mom and dad were two busy people; so, they hired workers to help with the house and the ground duties. Meals mattered in our house, and Ms. Letha helped to make our meals usually happy times. We ate suppers in an atmosphere of warm and comforting conversations. I was taught how and when to use the correct utensils, but mom didn't over complicate things.

Often, we had guests over for meals, and Mom was particularly conscientious about how and what was being served on those occasions. Food brought us together in a way that nothing else could have.

There was an exchange of recipes between the teachers at my mom's school. It was almost as if the educators had a garden club. They even went to the extent of sharing garden foods and dispensing seeds for the next garden year.

Some of the teachers traveled widely, and those who did not venture with them, did so through new food discoveries and explorations of the palate.

Many of the colored educators in the eastern part of North Carolina traveled to Columbia University in New York City's Upper Manhattan to study for their higher-level degrees: masters' degrees, or even doctoral degrees in education. They were proud peoples who returned with much knowledge. They sang the praises of Columbia University: Columbia University is a private Ivy League research university in Upper Manhattan, New York City. It was established in 1754 as King's College by royal charter of George II of Great Britain. Columbia is the oldest college in New York State and the fifth chartered institution of higher learning in the country, making it one of nine colonial colleges founded before the Declaration of Independence. A 1787 charter placed the institution under a private board of trustees before it was renamed Columbia University in 1896 when the campus was moved from Madison

Avenue to its current location in Morningside Heights occupying 32 acres (13 ha) of land. Columbia is one of the fourteen founding members of the Association of American Universities and was the first school in the United States to grant the M.D. degree.

When mom left for Columbia University, I was only six or seven years old. She left me in the hands of Ms. Letha when she left to study for her master's in education. I trotted behind Ms. Letha each day as she cleaned our house. I would ask her a string of questions, and sometimes she would answer; but sometimes, she turned the tables, and gave me a question to my question. At other times, she just grunted.

My inquisitiveness was much a part of me, as I asked, "Where does the sun go when we can't see it?"

Ms. Letha's arm was going to and fro across the ironing board when she replied, "Behind the clouds, I guess."

As Ms. Letha's slim body was taking the clothing down the hallway, my tiny legs moved behind her, and I asked, "Where do babies come from, Ms. Letha?"

Without wavering, she said, "Talk to your mother about that."

I could not allow myself to be shut off by her quick answers, so I continued, "Where is your husband, Ms. Letha?"

At first, her eyes avoided mine, and then she somberly said, "I don't have a husband."

Out of nowhere, I asked, "Why?"

Ms. Letha's eyes looked glassy, as if she was about to cry. After a few moments, when she answered, her words were slightly slurred, and she held her chest as if in pain. "Some of us can't keep our husbands," she finally announced.

I knew I asked a lot of questions and adults often paid no attention, telling me to go play, or not bother them right now, or some such. I had come to expect that attitude, but there was so much I wanted to know! So, I kept my questions inside my head until I was with this lady, Ms. Letha, who satisfied me with her answers, or at the very least -----pleased me with her expressions.

When she didn't answer, my words became a siren song, and I could see Ms. Letha rolling her pleasing eyes, and then she would exclaim, "Why do you ask so many questions, gal?"

Mom would come back from New York City loaded with gifts. She didn't forget a friend, husband, or child. In front of me, she unpacked pencils, pens, stationery, plates, and clothing with pictures of the Empire State Building printed boldly on each. I had my pick, but at the same time, I was told to think of others.

When I got older, I would spend time outside with dad and the yardman. Mr. Hester's face was mostly gloomy in contrast to that of my Ms. Letha. When I allowed myself to ask a question, the shy looking man would just snigger, showing his sparse teeth that were covered with tobacco stains. Then, he would let go a long stream of tobacco spit. I thought, "He could probably win a spitting contest," but then, it came to me that there was no such contest, not as I knew of anyway.

Then, there was a bunch of people who worked on our tobacco crop. My dad would pick them up in our almost new truck from the time the tobacco was planted in the spring until fall, when the dried tobacco was sold at the warehouse. The Bolder family and a few outsiders would hop from the truck one by one. Whenever they got glimpse of me, they would stare. Mom did not work in the field. She had too many other things to do. When I was not at school, I was with mom, dad, or Ms. Letha. That was before I met my additional family—the Bloomfields.

~~~~~~~~~~

Our circle consisted of families of Negro teachers, principals, undertakers, store owners, barbers, hairdressers, preachers, one dentist, and one doctor. Most of the peoples in the group needed assistance with their businesses, and that work was often done by the colored who were less educated. I had the opportunity to meet Mr. Bloomfield when he got a ride to work with my dad. Ida Lee Bloomfield and I became best friend when we were in grade school. The rest of her family embraced me with love and integrity as I became a part of their family.

Certainly, my parents were happy that I had such wonderful friends and a family that she trusted. When I knew I was going to visit Ida Lee, I would anxiously wait to wade through their flower garden, play with their cats and dogs, collect eggs from the hen's nests, and all the exciting things that happened in Jasper, North Carolina.

One Saturday, Mr. Bloomfield took us to the air show. We were guided down the highway, walking in a line behind the leader. Traffic on the highway was not constant until the weekend.

Mrs. Bloomfield was a very spiritual lady, and she tried to be tough. She believed that all fun things were a sin, such as dancing, going to movies, wearing make-up, playing sports, wearing shorts, and on and on. She had an ice cream heart, and I loved her all the more when she relaxed. That's when she would show her sweet and tender side.

Once when I visited, the lady let us go strawberry picking. The sky blurred blue, and the strawberry plants stretched out before us like a red and green woven piece of brocade. The taste of the berries overpowered us, and we ate until our stomachs popped. Now, Ida Lee and Mae Etta would not have eaten that many berries had I not encouraged them. We carried only a few berries back to the house, and I could tell that Ida Lee and Mae Etta were a little nervous about the situation.

My friends did not stand around their mother. They made a quick turn-around and proceeded outside. In no time, we were out in the flower garden. I was twitching and turning, while trying to reach the itchy spot in the calf of my leg. I was not conscious of how long I had been scratching. When I twisted my neck toward the back of me and got a glimpse of vivid red skin, I screamed, "My leg is on fire!"

All eyeballs were on my leg as I was escorted into the

house.

Once in the house, everyone crowded me to take a look, while I continued to twist and turn from the tingling sensation. My screaming brought Mrs. Bloomfield to my side.

While elbowing the others to the side, she said, "Y'all move outa' the way, so I can see what's goin' on here. Let me see."

She was quiet while she diagnosed the case.

I put my leg up high, so that she could see. "See, See!" I screamed.

Mrs. Bloomfield used her quiet voice, announcing, "You have been bitten by chiggers!" She seemed to collect her thoughts; and then she rushed to the cupboard in the kitchen and got a couple of items. Quickly dashing and rubbing, I could feel the discomfort lessening. In no time, the chigger bites had subsided to just an annoying sting.

Mr. Joey Bloomfield was not just a dad, but a male parent who was always there for us. With vim, vigor, and vitality, he spent his time shaping and challenging us whenever he could squeeze in the time. All of us had much respect and love for him. When I visited, I was ready and waiting to hear some of his hard time stories, but his children had heard them so many times, they were not ready to listen. They squirmed around as I listened to him tell about how he skimped and saved to buy his first bicycle and later his repair kit and air pump. With a broad grin that stretched straight across his face from left ear lobe to right ear lobe, he recounted the story of him and his friend, Garfield, building a small house for him and his bride, Amma. He proudly said, "Me and Garfield built this house with just a hammer, nails and a saw, and all of our materials came from the woods, or were leftovers. We got the unused bricks from the brickyard."

Mom and Dad were so happy for the assistance of the Bloomfield family. It took a village to work at our self-esteem which had been crushed by the schizophrenia of segregation that had demonized the world. Prominence, education, and ownership of property did not buy our way out of the chaos of segregation. Needless to say, to the whites, we "all" were *"just"* colored folks, and none of us were people.

I was very curious, and very nosy about sex. When I got my hands on a romance novel, I'd read it through and through, and, then passed it on to Ida Lee. When I visited her, we'd watch the farm animals and made analogies based on what we had read and what the other children had told us.

You might say that I had a wild streak in me. My mom and dad could see the ghost and would call me their "angel child". "When the name did not fit me just right, my parents decided to send me to Palmer Institute. I started the school at the beginning of my freshman high school year, 1952.

Palmer Institute was founded by Charlotte Hawkins Brown who was born in Henderson, North Carolina in 1883. The family migrated to Boston in 1888. The Hawkins and many other families thought they had a greater chance to gain economic, political, social, and educational opportunities in Boston. In that northern city, Charlotte met Alice Freeman Palmer who mentored her over the years. Later, when Charlotte returned to the South, Palmer supported her idea of building and incorporating an educational institution that would offer opportunities for young black/African-American students, who were hungry for educational opportunities.

The school began as a rural African-American School, in Sedalia, North Carolina and was named for Brown's mentor, Alice Freeman Palmer. The curriculum development at the school was influenced by the subjects Brown had taken at her schools in Cambridge, Massachusetts. While in grammar school, Ms. Brown took subjects that were guarded by the recommendations of the National Education Association. By the time Brown went off to high school, she was familiar with such classic as: *Robinson Crusoe, Swiss Family Robinson* and *Black Beauty* and had memorized works by esteemed writers such as Emerson, Longfellow, Whittier, and many others.

Palmer Institution provided cultural training, where we participated in supervised hikes, parties, and socials. Closely supervised proms and informal dances were common. All students participated in physical education. Boys' basketball, football, and baseball teams competed with teams from other schools, and girls played basketball. We attended activities with other schools including, Bennett College, North Carolina Agricultural and Technical College (A&T), and Dudley High School. Seniors were afforded an opportunity to take a ten-day trip to a northern city. Students who needed to off-set expenses could work on campus up to four hours a day as janitors, grounds keepers, farmhands, or kitchen and dining hall helpers.

Ms. Brown emphasized truth, beauty, and goodness, and the school offered a fully accredited course of study with special voice, piano, orchestra, dramatics, and art. There were multiple glee clubs for the students. However, the boys enjoyed singing in their quartette groups.

Palmer was a distinctive school of Christian culture, and it also instilled a little bit of New England in the character of its North Carolina students. Our faith was strengthened through weekly prayer meetings, Sunday school and church services, daily and Sunday vespers, and mandatory morning chapel attendance.

There was a restriction on the mixing of sexes. An invisible line divided girls' and boys' areas on campus. We were separated at chapel, various assemblies, and off campus trips. The sexes studied at the library on separate nights. The girls in particular were restricted and protected. We were not allowed to enter the country store across the street from the school if boys were there. The young ladies were weighed regularly and examined by a doctor ---Brown's secreted way of detecting pregnancy.

Personal appearance was considered extremely important. Groups of students were divided by age and sex for faculty adviser meetings, where we received training in cleanliness, health and hygiene, appropriate dressing—always neatly and tastefully, good posture, and so forth. The dress code, which was implemented as early as 1907, still existed when I entered in 1952, and remained the same as I graduated in 1956.

Our studies were very important. Teachers supervised a mandatory two-hour period for four or five nights a week. Boys were allowed to call on girls once or twice a month. Kissing was a serious offense. Card playing was not permitted.

~~~~~~~~~~~

Courageously, I returned home after graduation to assist my family with the farm, while Ida Lee went off to work in Washington, DC. Still, I felt that she had remained my best girl-friend, even though, we had been apart for five years.

During grade school, we had stuck together through thick and thin. My mother would always pack my lunch with fruits and sandwiches. She would use a brown lunch bag and wax paper for my sandwiches, while Addie had peanut butter crackers with no wrapping. Very soon, I had my mother to make two lunches. Ida Lee discontinued bringing a lunch, and we provided the lunch until I left for Palmer Institute.

Now she was coming home for Mae Etta's graduation, and I could vividly remember all the good times I shared with her and the Bloomfield family. I was aware that I had been blessed to be one of the students to attend such quality, prestigious school, as Palmer Institute. I did appreciate all that I had been taught, and I felt that I was a better person after my four years. It was my desire that the precious memories would always be indelibly printed on my brain. I was anxious to visit the Bloomfields and share all about my stay at Palmer Institute.

On my return, the Bloomfield family greeted me with hugs and kisses. Ida Lee was still the kind and thoughtful person she had been back in Pleasant Hill Elementary School. Mae Etta had grown up to be a beautiful young lady. Robert was a wide-eyed handsome boy, but, oh, how I missed Buddy! You might say that he was the class clown, who always kept us laughing. However, the amazing part of the reunion was the appearance of little Christine. She came to the family while I was away in school. *"Miracles do happen!"* I thought.

When Mrs. Bloomfield went to the kitchen to prepare the food and Mr. Bloomfield disappeared outside, I asked quietly, "Do you really want to hear some good stories about Palmer Institute?"

Everyone seemed to perk up their ears, while they drew their chairs close me. Robert sat cross-legged on the floor, while little Christine sat on Ida Lee's lap. I let them know how wonderful my stay at school really was, but I also let them know that we were demanded to follow rules. I continued, "Dormitory rules were posted in the rooms, on bulletin boards, and elsewhere but we found a way to do what we wanted. We did sneak out to play cards behind the dormitories."

Mae Etta asked, with astonishment, "You all did?"

"Why yeah, girl," I said, while trying to hold a straight face.

Giggling, she asked, "Did you have a boyfriend?"

While grinning, I inquired, "What do you think?"

Laughter tittered around the room. Mae Etta and Ida Lee said in unison, "I think you did! You did! Didn't you Anna?"

"Sure, I did," I said, as I felt a sheepish grin roll across my lips.

Even Christine was doing a baby laugh and clapping her little hands.

I finally said, "We even did some kissing."

Everyone started clapping and laughing. When Mae Etta regained her voice, she stated, "Tell us about that."

I was feeling just swell being the center of attention. I had a gift for holding a group's attention. That was the story of my life. I sat straight in my chair, cleared my throat, and announced, "Well, let me tell you all," and just then, I bent over laughing

Everyone was clapping, laughing and some were doubled over in tears.

Robert rolled on the floor while laughing. Baby Christine, who would be two years-old in two weeks, was laughing and showing her two teeth in her mouth.

I felt that we all had a well-deserved laugh; so, I cleared my throat again and wiped my runny eyes on my sleeve, sat up straight and made another announcement, "For real, I'm going tell you all this time. We did kiss behind the dormitory."

Then it occurred to me, that maybe, I was saying too much around the younger ones. I paused, and then said, "Just kidding."

Mae Etta knew better. She raised her eyebrows, and said, "No you ain't."

Ida Lee had regained her prim and proper way of sitting, and was asking very few questions, but she knew that I would tell her all the details later, when the others were not around.

"How did you get punished?" Mae Etta asked, as if she was planning to attend the school.

"Well, what I had to do was to work in the dining room for two weeks," I said, as if it was no big deal.

Everyone sat and looked at me. I could tell that they were enjoying every delicious scoop.

I hadn't finished, anyway. I was having the time of my life. I continued, "Now, let me tell you this: You know what?"

Everyone looked wide-eyed and ready, as some said, "Wha-a-at?

I let out a breath of air and then declared, "The boys got in trouble, too."

Robert had gotten in the groove. He asked, "What trouble?"

I answered, "Trouble, like, for sleeping through assemblies and playing betting games on things like, how long vesper would last, or how Ms. Brown would deal with a certain bad behavior."

"A-a-a-h," Robert managed to say with a frown, and then he asked, "What's assemblies and vespers?"

I had always admired Ms. Brown, and now I was feeling like I was she. Since, I was the teacher of the group, I stood, and said, "Boys and girls, assembly is when we get together in a room, hall, or any place we want. And vesper is just like church . . . to me." I humped my shoulders and spread my hands.

Robert seemed to be really thinking it all through, but an

"Uh-u-u-huh," finally came out of his mouth.

Mae Etta took over and asked, "What were the boys' punishments?

Before I could answer, she asked, "Were they like the girls?"

"Oh! They had to work on the grounds or in the vegetable fields for a few weeks," I said. While waiting for another question, Christine wiggled off Ida Lee's lap. She tottered out of the room. Watching her walk was so delightful, and none of us wanted to miss the scene. We all jumped up and ran behind the baby.

Stairs to Yonder

6 CHAPTER SIX

MAE ETTA

The function of education is to teach

one to think intensively and to think critically.

Intelligence plus character-

that is the goal of true education.

~ Dr. Martin Luther King

Beyond the excitement of graduation, our graduating class was also taking an extended educational trip to Washington, D.C. As we boarded our bus on an April morning, a classmate, Bill, asked to sit beside me. That was my pleasure, so I gave him a charming smile, and said, "Hu-huh."

Adding to our excitement was the rain that did a dance on the windshield. The wipers made music that was barely heard over the chattering young men and ladies. Bill really had a great understanding of small talk. Yet, he was not unaware of my charm. As time went by, we moved a fraction closer, and then close to each other.

All year, we had done extensive studies and researches on the places we would be visiting in the capital city. We had learned that the states of Maryland and Virginia each donated land to form the federal district. The district was named in honor of George Washington, one of the United States' founding fathers, and the first President of the United States of America.

We even read and studied about some of the famous men who had been monumentalized in the district. One of these was Thomas Jefferson, a founding father, a principal author of the Declaration of Independence and the third President of the United States. Another was Abraham Lincoln, who was the 16th president, and one who spoke out against slavery. Of course, there were others.

After a smooth ride, we arrived in Washington, D.C. We found our hotel and disembarked. My first night at a hotel was an overwhelming experience.

The next morning, we had breakfast and later visited the United States Capital. We had our picture taken on the steps of the Capital, as each class had done before us. Moving on, Bill and I held hands and squeezed fingers as we went on to see the Washington Monument and then, the Lincoln Memorial with Abraham Lincoln, who seemed to be looking at us.

In the month of April, the cherry blossoms were at their peak. They created an unforgettable sea of pink and white. We were reminded not to pick the blossoms. It was against the law.

We were told that the cherry trees were presented to the United States in 1912, while William Taft was president. The blossoms represented a close bond that was forged between the United States and Japan. The presenter was Tokyo Mayor Yukio.

When our first day was over, we were exhausted from all the walking and getting on and off our bus at our many stops throughout our busy day. We headed back to the hotel and spent our second night.

The next day, we spent most of our day visiting what we nick-named "another world," the Smithsonian Institution. The numerous displays were overwhelming.

The next morning, we loaded the bus to return home. Our class trip to Washington, D. C. had opened up a whole new world for the class of 1957. Association and bonding between classmates took place on that trip, and never would had happened otherwise. We all grew closer as the result of that experience. Bill had blessed my trip with love and caring.

On the way home, the rain did not let up during our return trip, but at least it did not wreak havoc on our traveling. We arrived back at Newbold Training School safely.

~~~~~~~~~~~

On the most perfect day in May, the sunlight burst through the window. I got out of bed to make preparation to begin my journey to the High school.

After washing up, I made way to the kitchen for breakfast. "Good morning, Mama," I almost sang, and began to assist her with the frying ham in the skillet, as she slid the pan of biscuits into the oven. Mama raised her eyebrows and smiled as she spoke. Seemingly, she had an uplifted spirit in spite of the fact that a number of her children had already left home, and another one was on the way out. As the family came in for breakfast, everyone seemed to be happy and pleased about the upcoming event of the day.

We still didn't own a vehicle, so we again waited patiently for the uncle to take us to Dover. After a seemingly long wait, I became restless and couldn't sit still, so I paraded outside and stood by the front door where the sunshine greeted me. The warmth of the sun caused me to perspire, and my hair began to puff, so I quickly returned to the indoors, where I sat with the family.

A while later, my Uncle Roy drove up in his new 1957, blue and white Chevy. Mama's brother bought a new car every year, and he was very generous about taking us places. The gorgeous day stood out before us as we drove down highway 55, passing by two white schools, Jasper High, and Fort Barnwell High. The car was crammed with my entire family. I sat huddled in a cramped position in the back seat. I closed my eyes while silently repeating my salutatorian address. Mrs. Rouse, my English teacher worked diligently with me on the piece of scholarly work. Mama would be proud of me even if I would make a mess, but my teacher wanted excellence from her students and would accept nothing less. I prayed that I would not disappoint my family or Mrs. Rouse.

When we reached school, there were many unknown cars in the parking area. Usually, there were only the principal's and teachers' cars occupying their given spaces. The janitor, who also did pickup services, drove a truck. The students were aware of each person's car. On a given day, if the car was not in its designated spot, perhaps that particular teacher was not at school. Over time, we learned that sometimes the teacher or principal would ride with another teacher, which meant that we had to wait until we got inside to get the true answer.

We drove around holes, trying to find a decent parking spot. When the rain came, the holes were full of water. The school system would send someone out to fill the pot holes at the "Negro Schools" every once a while.

Entering the school building, my family made their way down the hall to the cafeteria, which was also used as an auditorium.

I went to the classroom where all the graduates were waiting. Bill was waiting for me with a note between his fingers. After all, we had spent some time sharing our dreams and aspirations. However, it seemed that after we returned to Newbold Training High, our light, fluffy romance was over.

I joined the girls that seemed to have been engaged in girl talk. Everyone was overflowing with happy memories, and I could feel the melancholy that lingered throughout the room. We all seemed to realize that we were at a crossroad and were centering on probabilities and possibilities.

Mrs. Rouse and the principal, Mr. Redder, came into the room, and had us line up just the way we had practiced. We lined up from the shortest to the tallest, girls first. When we reached the cafeteria-auditorium, all the graduates marched to the front seats that were reserved just for them. The valedictorian and salutatorian continued to the stage to join the superintendent and other school administrators. Making my way to the stage was not easy. My heart fluttered wildly as I approached the steps, and my knees felt like rubber.

To be on stage was impressive, and I could feel Mama and Daddy's eyes on me, but in a weird way, I desired to be in the audience with my classmates.

The auditorium was packed to capacity, and everyone was looking his or her best. Families were out to see their young ladies or young men graduate from high school. For many, the graduate was the first in the family; so, having a high school graduate in the family was considered a great honor for the African-American families.

Personal appearance was considered extremely important when we attended any school function. The ladies were beautifully dressed, wearing hats and high-heeled shoes, with matching purses. Some even carried gloves. The men wore suits, heavy ones, even though, the weather was quite warm, as the month was May. Most of the men only had one suit, and it was worn year-round.

Thirty-four graduates had marched into the auditorium. Each one had a place in the world. We were aware that there would be many intersections ahead, and we would have to make choices. Over the years, under the tutelage of our faithful teachers and the principal at New Bold Training School, we had gained the basic skills necessary to succeed as we moved on down our own roads.

Greetings and congratulations came from the mouth of the salutatorian as she addressed the graduates, while the valedictorian said farewell, goodbye and Godspeed.

7 CHAPTER SEVEN

JOEY

"All the great things are simple,

and many can be expressed in a single word:

freedom, justice, honor,

duty, mercy, hope."

~ Winston Churchill

On a sunny day, in the late spring of 1957, right after Mae Etta's graduation, Berman paid me a visit. I was piddling around in my vegetable garden as he entered the gate. I noticed that his big brown eyes gave off excitement as he spoke, "How are you doin' Joey?"

"Fine! Fine! What would bring you here?" I said, in one big breath.

"I gotta' go somewhere this afternoon, and I want you to go with me," he announced.

I could feel the excitement without hearing where we were going. Berman always found extraordinary things to do and exceptional places to go. For the most part, my going along with Berman, insured me of gaining more wisdom and understanding.

"Well, hear this," he said, "my minister and many other

black ministers are meeting at New Bold Training High School tonight. They are meeting with an organization called SCLC, and they would even like for the church congregations and visitors to attend."

"SCLC, huh," was all I could think of saying.

"Now, I don't exactly know what the letters stand for, but we'll find out when we get there. Wanta' go?"

I gave a big chuckle as I said, "Now, Berman, if you say go, I'll sho' go. Man, you know where to go and when to go."

We both bent over laughing, as we patted each other on the back.

Berman stood and gave me a serious look- over, and said, "Now, man, we have got to look good. We will be meeting with these big-time preachers, mostly from the Baptist Churches."

"What'd I wear," I asked.

"Yo' best suit, man. What else?" Berman said.

"U-u-u-h, my best suit may not be good enough for the big-time preachers," I said, with a teasing grin. However, Berman knew me; I always felt good in whatever I had on.

Berman stretched his arm and pushed his sleeve up to look at the time on his watch. Then he said, "I'll be back to get you in 'bout two hours." He then rushed off.

I went in to talk to Amma about our meet up at the school.

In about two hours, Berman was back. I was ready, dressed in my only Sunday suit, but feeling dapper.

I was taught that habitual lateness was showing disrespect for others, so I had impressed upon myself the need to always be on time. Remembering what I had been taught by my grandma, I rushed out to Berman's car as soon as he showed up.

On the way to the meeting, I asked Berman if he had heard anything about Sadie.

Berman said that he did hear something at church on Sunday.

I asked, "Is she with her brother, Henry?"

"Sally Jones said that she is staying with her sister in Lenoir

County," Berman told me.

"I'm glad she went to stay with Lillie," I stated.

"I never did know Lillie. She got any children?" Berman asked.

I had to think. Then I said, "I think she got two girls."

"I miss her a lot," I said, and Berman knew exactly what I meant. However, things had cooled off a bit, since she had gotten older.

We arrived at the meeting when everyone was congregating. Berman introduced me to his pastor, Reverend Paul Smith, a tall, dark skinned, middle-aged man.

The Reverend, in turn, introduced us to many other people: ministers, deacons, sisters, brothers, and seemingly everybody he knew. We talked until someone asked us to come to order.

Reverend Paul Smith was the master of ceremonies. He was quite polished, with a deep voice and clear pronunciation. Peering over his glasses, he introduced the ministers on the dais, and then got down to business. Right away, he gave us the name of the organization: the "Southern Christian Leadership Conference."

The ministers on the dais pointed out in no uncertain terms that Martin Luther King, Jr. and Ralph Abernathy felt the need for an organization that would involve the black churches in the South. They went on to say that in this year of 1957, (and President Dwight Eisenhower, "Ike" was in his second term in 1957), we were still waiting for a change in our conditions in the southern states in these United States. The government was all promises and no action. In the South, blacks were still segregated from whites in schools and most other public places and services. We were kept from voting by poll taxes, literacy tests, grandfather clauses, and intimidation tactics. Social segregation remained the cause of our being poorly educated, while economic discrimination kept us in a state of perpetual poverty.

Then it was said that many of us decided to change demographics. We took our chances and moved North. Some

African-Americans received assistance from the National Urban League. The league's motto was, *"Not Alms, But Opportunity."* The Urban League's creed reflected its emphasis on self-reliance and economic advancement.

Reverend Thomas Simmons was a short, light brown skinned young man who was dressed immaculately. He had the pleasure of working with King and Abernathy when the organization was in the planning stage. He gave us the rudiments of this newest organization.

"Martin Luther King, Jr., Ralph Abernathy, and sixty ministers and civil rights activists founded the Southern Christian Leadership Conference. They recognized the need for a national organization to help with our efforts to assist those African-Americans who have no desire to move North. They have their roots in their home place in the South. They have the desire to do for themselves what they rightly expected their government to do.

King felt that the harnessing of the moral authority and organizing the power of black churches would help conduct non-violent protests to promote civil rights reform. His participation in the organization would give him a base of operation throughout the South, as well as a national platform. The organization felt the best place to start to give African-Americans a voice was to enfranchise them in the voting process and . . ."

At the point that *"voting"* was mentioned, I could feel my heart squeeze, as I remembered a voting incident that my granddaddy had told me about. I felt that so much had been done, but from where I stood, *no* progress had been made. I then looked over at Berman. His bottom lip was drooped, and his brown eyes were deep and luminous as he listened.

I tightly pressed my lips together and my mind drifted off. I looked around and noticed heads bobbing, hands were lifted, and the "Amens" were loud and clear. Suddenly, I felt strongly encouraged, as I thought, "Just maybe we could make a breakthrough."

Bringing my mind back into focus, I became aware of the change of speakers. Before us, stood another colored man with a loud voice. He sure wanted us to hear what he had to say; he continued:

The founders of the SCLC organization and the many ministers throughout the South, who were organizing with this newest African-American organization, were well aware of the value of other civil rights organizations that were founded in the first decade of the 20th century. There was the Niagara Movement, where W.E.B. DuBois met with a group of black intellectuals in Niagara Falls, Canada. Their goal was to find ways for securing equal rights for blacks.

Later, W.E.B. DuBois, other members of the Niagara Movement, and a group of white progressives founded the National Association for the Advancement of Colored People, better known as NAACP. Their mission was to abolish all forms of segregation and to increase educational opportunities for African-American children. A few years before 1957, The National Association for the Advancement of Colored People (NAACP), guided by its chief lawyer, Thurgood Marshall, decided to use Brown v. Board of Education and its companion cases to challenge the "separate but equal" principle. Supreme Court Chief Justice Earl Warren read the court's opinion in the case of Brown v. Board of Education. The court, in a unanimous decision, decided that separate schools- for blacks and whites - was unconstitutional.

Berman and I were members of the NAACP, but tonight we were learning even more about the organization's history.

The meeting at the schoolhouse was deep and extensive in content, and the discussions were meaningful. Most people felt that all students should be able to go to their own neighborhood schools. Students would not have to ride a bus for long distances in order to attend a segregated school.

We were reminded that the struggle to integrate schools

and public facilities would be long and difficult; our leaders at the meeting impressed upon us that we would need to keep our wits about us, have energy and the willingness to press forward without violence, no matter what might happen.

The meeting concluded with scriptures and prayers. Both were comforting and promising, but one thing was for sure, the ministers did not want us to get caught up in an endless cycle of violence and vengeance.

When the meeting was over, there was an outburst of generous handclapping. We then gathered in bunches, sounding like buzzing bees.

Afterward, we made our way out the door, into the dimly lit parking lot, and to the car. Berman and I just sat in the car for a little while, sorting through our thoughts.

Finally, I said, "We sure have a lot of work to do if we want our children to have a better life than we have had."

Berman scratched his chin, as he replied, "We sho' do." Then he cranked up the car, and we rode off.

After riding for a while in silence, I said what I was thinking, "Maybe, we will make a breakthrough."

Keeping his eyes straight ahead, Berman mumbled, "Just *maybe.*"

We were silent for minutes. Then Berman spoke, "This nation seems to be determined to keep us under foot."

I did not see a light at the end of the tunnel. I took a deep breath to comfort myself, then finally found the courage to say,"I guess we have to believe."

"Yes, believe that there is a God up there, and he will see us through," Berman said, repeating what some of the ministers had said at the meeting.

I said a strong, healthy, "Amen!"

Berman stopped at my house, and as I got out of the car, I wished him a, "Good night." I knew that I would not be so involved if it were not for Berman. He was a dear friend and a born and bred Baptist. I had visited his church. In fact, Ida Lee, Mae Etta, and Buddy had been immersed in the waters of the

Baptist Church.

My wife's father was a Baptist preacher. However, Amma, her mother, and her sisters, had joined the Church of God in Newport News, Virginia. They became staunch members of the church and believed that their way was the only way.

~~~~~~~~~~

When I entered the house, a brief smile flickered on Amma's face, and I allowed myself a small grin. My brain was crowded with all that I had heard. I was quiet while trying to organize my mind.

Amma asked, "How was the meeting?"

I told her how impressed I was with such a great organization, and how strongly encouraged I was feeling. I went on to explain the SCLC organization, and why it was formed.

Suddenly, I felt awkward. Amma didn't seem to be listening to me. In the quietness of the room, I removed my Sunday suit, hanging it in its proper place.

I glanced at Amma sitting there in her rocking chair, and I insisted on breaking the monotony. I stated, "When we attended the NAACP meetings, there were many white people. Black ministers brought along buses of their congregation."

Once more I looked at Amma, and she seemed strangely distracted. As I stood staring at her, she said, "Mae Etta wanta' go to work in New York City."

By that time, I had put on my old patched overalls. I said, "Huh, that's what she wanta' do, huh? We'll have to talk about that." Then, I proceeded to the kitchen to check the water bucket. I should have guessed why Amma was so quiet. I had overheard them talking about the trip to New York a few days ago.

Once on the outside, I sat on the base of the pump, which was a perfect place for me to languish in my thoughts of Mae Etta going to a big city where she didn't know anyone. Scary things, that I wanted to let go of, were simmering in the back of my mind. The other two children went with family members that we knew. The kinfolks embraced the idea that my family was the love of my life. They were well aware that my children's love bore into me with pervasiveness like blood in my veins while working its way to the center of my heart.

Sitting there in the damp warm air, I looked skyward at the luminous moon hanging there in the night, and I decided right then and there that I would not let my emotions get the best of me. Nor was I going to let the agony of fear overpower me. I was going to use my emotions for good of all of us. I felt that, just maybe, it would be ok for Mae Etta to go away, up yonder, and get a job. After all, Mae Etta was in search of solace and dignity. She had not wavered in her determination to become a school teacher. I knew that I could not stand in her way. There was one thing for sure, I had to discuss the situation with Amma sooner and not later, and tonight would be sooner.

Once inside, I closed and hooked the back door, and then checked in on the children as I customarily did each night.

When I entered the bedroom, Amma was just finishing her scriptures reading for the night. She put her Bible down as if she were ready to talk.   I started where we had left off earlier in the evening, "So, Mae Etta wanta' go to work in New York City, huh?"

"Yeap, that's what she is planning on," Amma said, as she rocked back and forth in her rocking chair.

"And she gonna' stay with that old lady she been writing to?" I carefully asked.

Sounding very courageous, Amma said, "Yeap, done wrote and told her she was coming."

I was feeling less alarmed, as I said, "O-o-oh! Then she's gonna' go off to that big city all by herself?"

"Cain' nobody go with her. So, she gonna have to go by herself," Amma said, as if I was missing the point.

Amma didn't realize I had already accepted this reality. There were no jobs for African-Americans in our part of the country. So, the only thing to do was to move to where the jobs were.

"So, she wanta' go before the 'bacco season?" I inquired.

Amma took a deep breath and stood to face me, as she said, "She trying to get away from all that scum and dirt, and I don't much blame her."

"Well, I'll go to the bus station tomorrow, and find out how much the bus ticket is gonna cost to go to New York City," I said, as Amma was getting down on her knees to pray.

I got down beside her as she prayed aloud. She always had long and windy prayers, and tonight, it was no different. She sent up a humble plea, asking God to grant Mae Etta supreme blessedness and happiness. Raising her eyes to the ceiling, she begged of Him to go along with her and protect her every step of the way.

The night was very quiet, and as we lay in bed, Amma said, "I told Mae Etta to do as she was taught: be brave, have faith, and trust in the Lord."

I lay quiet, while I truly believed that my daughter had courage and conviction that was embedded deep in her chest. She was driven by a powerful hunger for learning and would make things happen.

Amma and I talked further into the night. With my eyes closed in the darkness, I said, "After I get enough money for the bus ticket, Mae Etta and you can set a day for her to leave."

"Yes, she will probably be at home the next two weeks," Amma said with a yawn.

I definitely felt that in two weeks, I could save enough for the cost of the ticket. So, I said, "Y'all just make the arrangements."

In a few minutes, I could hear Amma's snoring. It was only natural that she was completely satisfied and was having a very peaceful night. She had reminded me that we were not alone in making our decisions; God was with us.

I tried to comfort myself with the knowledge that Mae Etta would be better off working in New York City. I didn't feel worried, but I could not sleep.

After counting a few sheep, I got out of bed. I opened the curtains and the moonlight illuminated through the window. I raised the window a little higher than it once was. The fresh air smelled better than my roasted peanuts. I took in a deep breath, went back to bed, and was asleep in no time.

~~~~~~~~~~

Daylight came quickly—too quickly. I didn't feel exactly rested, but I lifted my jaded body out of bed. The radiant sun peeked through the trees, while the birds made joyful noises outside. They seemed to remind me to be considerate about Mae Etta's trip. Keeping her at home would be like keeping her down, which meant she could not soar as she otherwise might. Even though she was a part of me, I should realize that she should not remain in the nest. Remembering that I had to get enough money for the trip, I quickened my steps to get ready for work.

The fire in the stove roared, and on top, the coffee pot rocked with steam spewing from its spout. I grabbed a light breakfast, guzzled down my coffee, and was on my bike going to work on what was left of the farm. Of course, the few farm animals had to be fed, and Sam needed me to carry out other duties. At the same time, I needed the money to buy the bus ticket for my daughter.

Amma kept her wits about her and did some serious juggling. After two or three weeks, we thought we had saved enough money for the bus ticket, but I would have to go into town to get the cost.

Summer was just around the corner, and the weather was getting hot. As on most Saturdays, I stood beside the highway, thumbing a ride to town. The traffic was moderately heavy with familiar and unfamiliar travelers. Most of them were happy to give me a ride. Others seemed oblivious of my need and looked straight ahead as they went by. Whether we were acquaintances, or not, the rides were mostly pleasant with good conversation.

I always had the manners and willingness to oblige the person who had been considerate enough to give me a lift. Some refused to accept payment, and others would quote an amount. There was a couple of times that the price of my ride left me embarrassingly little for shopping. No matter what, I would meet my obligations.

The bus traveled the highway, but it came later in the day. We preferred getting into town early and returning on the afternoon bus. Therefore, getting home before the afternoon squalls came up. They brought on cracks of lightning and rumbles of thunder.

On this particular Saturday, I did not want to venture downtown. The main purpose of my journey to town was to get a ticket for the trip to New York City, but while I was there, I bought as many staples as I could afford.

After shopping, I stood around in Five Points, talking with acquaintances. Voices flew back and forth, up, down, and across the streets. During the commingling, we gathered lots of news, from talking about the president, Dwight Eisenhower, to chatting about the weather. Much of the news was old and stale, but we had no way of hearing about the happenings early on. We got them when and how we could. Newspapers were unheard of in our neck of the woods. We depended on the radio if we owned one and if we had time to listen.

Five Points was just an ordinary place, but with the many stores and shops that had colored owners, the few blocks had become an extraordinary place. Saturday had become the magical day for some to mill around and others to do some shopping, while rich, soulful music amplified throughout the area.

Five points had become a meeting place for the young on Saturday nights. The Marines from the Cherry Point Airbase were seen among the gatherings.

Time had come for me to move toward the bus station. I dismissed myself, and later found myself on the crowded bus, returning home. We, colored folks, were crammed in the back like sardines. When the bus was just a little ways from my house, I pulled the rope that had a bell sound. The driver slowed down, but he stopped a little ways past my dwelling. In the meanwhile, I slid up the aisle, guiding my burlap sack in front of me.

I stepped off the bus in front of the grounds where the old home- place house once stood. A red truck sat in the driveway. On the plot, stood a man who seemed to be wearing work clothes that resembled a construction worker. I put my sack by the mailbox as I walked over to him. The young man had a generous smile with a thin red face. Thick glasses stuck to his nose. He removed his cap and smoothed his thin, wiry hair as he spoke, "Aunt Sadie wants us to look in to constructing her a new house."

I gasped, "Huh! O-o-oh!" It was obvious that I was surprised. So, I took a deep breath, and then asked, "When? Where?"

"We thought this spot might be ok," he said, pointing his stubby fingers at a spot opposite the debris that still lay there. The place was even more overgrown with weeds and dandelions.

I bit my tongue, and said, "Ok, my house is right over there. See you around."

The sun was a bright orange ball as I moved toward my sack. Lifting it from the ground, I threw it over my shoulder and moved toward my house with the sack riding my back.

During the evening, Amma and I traded thoughts, ideas, and opinions about Sadie having a house built.

"I'm thinking Sadie shoulda' said something to us 'bout it befo' now," Amma had said.

"She's the same ole Sadie, even after all she's been through," I surmised.

Getting a new house on our property was on our minds, but we had more important business to discuss.

I told Amma the price of the ticket to New York City.

"Oh my Lawd! We barely have enough," Amma said with

104

surprise. "That ticket sho' was high."

"Yeah, but that's a long ways to go," I said, giving the distance some thought.

"Mae Etta is all ready to travel. She has finished making her black gabardine skirt that she wanted to wear."

I couldn't resist as I said, "She's a smart girl."

With a smile lurking in her eyes that gradually spread to the rest of her face, Amma said, "You say that 'bout all your children at one time or another."

Amma went on to tell me that Mae Etta would be leaving for New York City in a week.

8 CHAPTER EIGHT

MAE ETTA

The greatest gifts

you can give your children

are the roots of responsibility

and the wings of independence.

~ Denis Waitley

Mama stared from a safe distance as I stepped on the stairs of the bus to yonder. I could feel her sinking world as we moved out of her sight. She had said, "Remember, you are taking a piece of all of us with you."

I clung to my shoebox of food while my money clung to my underwear. Mama had safety-pinned it in a secure fashion. As I began my journey, I was surprisingly titillated by the thoughts of all of the possibilities that might be before me. Suddenly, I sank into a daydream of how this all happened.

It all happened about two years ago. Mama had been a faithful subscriber to her church's newspaper ever since she first became affiliated. Within the covers of *"The Happy News"* were Bible puzzles and an invitation to write responsibly. I couldn't resist the puzzles or the other opportunities to express my ideas. Time and time again, I blissfully produced and presented my best, and then, anxiously waited for the outcome in the upcoming issue of the newspaper. Having very few books and no magazines or other newspapers in our house, I was ecstatic when *"The Happy News"* arrived.

One of the members from the Church of God Congregation in New York City was so moved by my letter in the paper that she responded to me directly, writing a personal letter. From then on, we kept up a regular correspondence, writing to each other frequently.

Later, she sent me boxes of clothes and a typewriter. I made her aware of my upcoming graduation from high school and my status as an honor student. As time went by, I acknowledged the fact that I desperately wanted to go to college to become a school teacher, but that I was financially unable to do so.

She graciously invited me to come to New York after graduation. She seemed positive about my ability to find work. With my Mama and Dad's blessings, I accepted the invitation. I was taking a risk, but I was also choosing to trust in my positive instincts.

My Mama had repeated time and time again, "You are not alone; God is with you." As I rode toward New York, I was not afraid, and I did feel His presence.

My high school English teacher, Mrs. Rouse, and our supervisor, Mrs. Pugh, had given me books and brochures on the Black Colleges. I read them through and through and over and over. The pages that contained information about teachers' colleges were crimped and crinkled from use. Winston-Salem Teachers College was definitely my first choice. My intention was to work for one year and return to North Carolina for college.

My research had made me very knowledgeable about the school where I desired to spend four years of my life. I had indeed become an admirer of Dr. Simon Green Atkins. He was the founder of Winston-Salem Teachers College, and he oversaw the school's transition from a private to a state-controlled institution.

Atkins' parents were slaves, and he was the oldest child, born on June 11, 1863, in Chatham County, North Carolina. As a child, Atkins worked on a farm with his grandparents. As a young man, he studied under black educator pioneers, who came from St. Augustine's Normal Collegiate Institute. Later, the Institute became St. Augustine College, in Raleigh, North Carolina. One of his great mentors was the educational pioneer, Anna Julia Cooper, who was known for her work as an activist, scholar, feminist, and school administrator in Washington, D.C.

Mr. Atkins graduated from St. Augustine College in 1884. After graduation, he was invited to work with the president of Livingston College. This was an institution that was supported by the African Methodist Episcopal Zion Church, located in Salisbury, North Carolina. Mr. Atkins joined the faculty under the leadership of Joseph Charles Price, the president of the college. Mr. Price was a renowned educator and orator.

Atkins worked at Livingston College for six years. He played a dual role, acting as an educator and as the treasurer of the college. During that time, he spent his summer months conducting Seminars for black teachers in various counties.

Simon Green Atkins was well known, and many educational institutions wanted a piece of him, but the town of Winston Salem lured him to the post of principal of the Depot Street School. This was North Carolina's largest public school for African Americans. He worked in this position for five years. During that time, his interest was stimulated by the North Carolina Negro Teachers' Association (NCNTA), a group that he had helped to organize in 1881. With the assistance of the group, Atkins began to direct a group of educators as they established the foundation for a standard black teachers' college in the state.

As time went by, Dr. Atkins intensified his efforts to build a school for African Americans. He sought assistance from the Winston Board of Trade, the Chamber of Commerce, and even the local white residents. Local support was outstanding and came in steadily. The black community donated $2,000 and R.J.

Reynolds Tobacco Company contributed $500.00. Atkins obtained 50 acres of land, and the backing of the Chamber of Commerce. That was the beginning of Winston-Salem Teachers College.

My mind was wrapped around getting into that college, and I became hypnotized by the thought of what would happen in a year's time. Ever since I could remember, my goal had been to become educated, but my research had put me on another level. I became entrenched in a personal time-capsule of my life pre-college, and I truly believed that my entrapment would endure until I entered the doors of a collegiate institution.

~~~~~~~~~~

I arrived in New York City with an empty shoebox, and without incident. I stepped off the bus, looking around at the pool of people whom surrounded me. I took a look above, into the New York skies. The bubonic gray clouds lowered toward the earth and covered every inch of the sky. They were lowering and threatening to burst. The claustrophobic sky seemed to have brought on a feeling of gloom, but it was easily shaken, as my eyes searched for someone who might be Sister Jason. The name "Sister" was the handle designated to the ladies in the Church of God.

Seconds later, I noticed a statuesque, gray-haired lady coming toward me. Like magic, I fell into this tall lady's arms. Strangely, I felt that I had known her forever. We had gained a bond of friendship through our letter writing.

Sister Jason's brown eyes stared at me as she told me how happy she was to have me come to stay with her for a while. We then made our way to collect my luggage. She held my hand as we made our way across the street to find the car. As I observed her hand, I noticed that our hands were the same shade of brown.

When we reached the big gray car, Elder Boone stepped out, giving me a firm handshake. He then opened the back door, and I crawled in. Closing the door on my side, he rushed around to open the door for Sister Jason.

A beautiful lady with a full head of coal black hair sat in the front seat. She turned around and introduced herself as Sister Boone, the minister's wife.

We left the parking lot and went pretty quickly through the busy streets of the city. Seemingly, each person wanted to talk to me, but I found it impossible to hear over the beeping and squeaking of the traffic. I stared out the window as I said my "yes or no" one word replies to their inquiries.

When we reached 167th Street, where I would be staying for at least the next year, Sister Jason slowly pulled herself out of the car. In the meantime, I sprang out and waited to gather my belongings from the trunk.

The lady, who had a slight slump, said her thanks to the driver and then looked expectantly at me, and I got the message. I said thank you to the man that would be my minister for the next year.

Sister Jason mentioned the fact that there were too many people sitting around on the stoop. So, I had already learned a new word—"stoop".

Clutching my suitcase, I followed Sister Jason up the steps. She opened the outside door, and we entered the vestibule. Inside, on the two opposite walls, were many mailboxes with names and numbers on them. Our box number was the same that I had written so many times—#4B. The older lady opened her mailbox with a select key from a bunch of keys that dangled from a ring she held tightly in her hand. Using another key, she opened the inner door, and we walked into the hallway on the first floor.

The sister gave me a strong suggestion that I should generally walk to and from the second floor, but since at the moment, we were carrying a suitcase, we would ride the elevator.

The elevator door slid open and a couple emerged, holding the door for us to enter. Inside the elevator, I rested my suitcase, but by the time I had release the handle, we were on the second floor. I grabbed my piece of luggage and hustled out the door behind the lady, who walked as briskly as she could to the door at the end of the hall. When she got to #4B, she selected another key from the batch and gently pushed the door open.

I had been in New York for a little while, and already, I had gone through changes. Of course, at our home in North Carolina, we didn't lock doors or mailboxes; therefore, we didn't carry a big key ring. Once or twice, Mama or Dad decided to lock the door, and no one could find the key. So, we closed the door and went on our way. Of course, no one would have entered except Goldie Locks, and we would have been delighted to have her. We had very little company at our place.

Sister Jason and I walked in to an area with a floral couch and coat hanger. In the corner, stood a stand of multifarious flowers. She removed her jacket and hat. I followed her through to the kitchen to the room that would be my bedroom. Everything was spick and span, which was a characteristic of my home back in North Carolina. I left my suitcase in the room, as she invited me to sit with her in the room with the couch.

We were face to face, and I was getting my first good look at Sister Nellie Jason. I guessed her age to be about seventy-five. She had thinning, long hair and lots of gray that distinguished her. She was wearing a beautiful matching skirt and sweater. She had on nice, comfy, black shoes.

I, on the other hand, was dressed like it was summer time, with an off-the-shoulder, soft, blue blouse and a black skirt of my own design. I felt good about my dress; however, the weather was a little breezy.

Sitting in the comfort of the room, we got more acquainted. Sister Jason asked, "Did you like the long ride on the bus?"

Shifting my position on the couch, I managed to say, "Yes ma'am."

A ghost of a smile swept over her face as she said, "Please do not say 'Yes Ma am' to me."

I said, "Okay."

Primping her mouth and looking disgusted, she said, "You must say yes or no to me."

"Yes," I said, hoping the hounding was over.

I noticed her eyebrows narrowing as she said, "Please speak in complete sentences. You are supposed to be a high school graduate."

As my eyes were filling with tears, I wished myself back in North Carolina, but I managed to snort, "Yes, I liked the ride on the bus."

She sensed my feeling and carried on light conversation, and I found that she was quite an interesting lady. When I spoke, I was very careful and gave great thought to how and what I said. I admired her expressions and clearly spoken words. Seemingly, her quality of speaking ranked far above her letter writing skills.

Anyway, she seemed to be a little moody, and made it known that she wanted to know more about me.

I, in turn, tried to impress her, while I carefully expressed the facts that I spoke French fluently, was a speed Greg Shorthand writer, and a speed typist.

The lady said, "That's good to know. Maybe, you might want to send your mother the Sunday Sermons."

I shifted in my seat, as a thought of deep appreciation flashed across my mind for my loving mama and dad who gave all they could, and also for my twelve years at school with excellent teachers, principals, and the county supervisor, Mrs. Pugh. They all cared a great deal and filled in the gaps in every way that they could.

In the meanwhile, I gracefully, sat up straight on the sofa. I felt a little teary. My heart skipped a beat when I realized how far I had come from all the bullying I had endured in the elementary grades.

After what seemed like a long time of silence, the lady stated that she had secured a job interview for me at Macy's Department Store on 34th Street.

"Mr. Loughton said that you could come down to meet him

as soon as you got into the city," is what I was hearing the lady say. The idea of securing a job interview so quickly was something that I'd never dreamed of.

Later, we had a light dinner with tuna salad sandwiches and mincemeat pie ---a kind of pie that I had never eaten.

Our knowledge about each other grew, as I was shown the bathroom and where I would find towels and washcloths. I had never been in a bathtub. At our house, we used wash basins.

I unpacked my suitcase while Sister Jason washed the dinner dishes. While hanging my clothes in the closet and putting my belongings into the drawers, my eyes scanned the room. With all of its neatness, the bedroom was pretty remarkable. Wall-to-wall carpet felt soft under my bare feet. The mahogany double bed looked comfortable. The huge furniture left little space in the room. Nevertheless, I was ecstatic about having a room all to myself for the first time.

When I finished unpacking, I joined Sister Jason, who was sitting in the spotless kitchen thumbing through a magazine. I sat down across from her.

She glanced up and smiled, and then she said, "Mae, let me tell you about life in the big city."

I said, "Yes ma'-. I mean, Yes."

Smiling, she stated, "When you walk down the street, put your street face on and hold your purse firmly under your arm. Keep your eyes open and try not to ride in a taxi. Many of these taxi people drive like they are schizophrenic. If possible, get a bus or take the subway."
I said, "Yes, I'll try."

She gave me an "okay" smile, and reiterated what she had said in her letter, "I won't charge you any rent as long as you are working toward an educational goal."

"Thank—you—for—that," I stumbled.

Since I had spent the night before on the bus, Sister Jason suggested that I get to bed early to be ready for an early start in the morning. She wanted me to start to work as soon as possible so I could immediately start to save money for college.

We said good night, both of us bubbling with excitement.

As I trudged toward the bathroom, Sister Jason stated, "Take your bath at night, so you won't have to get up so early in the morning."

I graciously said, "Yes, I'll do that."

"Your towel and washcloth are on the rack on the left side of the tub," she announced.

I said, "Yes, I'll find them."

"Good night," she said again.

"Good night," I replied again.

When I came back through the kitchen, Sister Jason had gone to her bedroom, so I tiptoed to my bedroom.

Before getting into bed, I pulled out my paper and pencil and wrote to my family:

Dear Mama and Dad,

I arrived in New York City safe and sound. I loved the bus ride. I spent most of my time reading about Winston-Salem Teachers College. I hope to be back in North Carolina next year to attend the college.

Hope you all are well and doing fine. I will be going to church on Sunday. I will take the sermons in shorthand and type them out on Sister Jason's typewriter. She does not have a telephone. If you want to call me, call Elder and Sister Boone's number: 1-111-000-1234.

I hope that I will get a job at Macy's Department Store. I will be going there tomorrow for an interview.

May God bless you all,

Mae Etta

After writing the letter, I felt so much better. I shed my robe and climbed into bed. Cozying up in the bed, I was ready for a good night sleep, but instead, I was restless. Never mind, when I dozed off, I was awakened by a clamor of squeaks, beeping, and firetrucks sounds. After a long while, I was having sweet dreams.

9 CHAPTER NINE

JOEY

"He who is not courageous

enough to take risks

will accomplish nothing in life."

~ Muhammad Ali

Morning came without the show of an early sunrise, and the chattering of birds was not heard. I was awakened by Sister Jason, as she stood in the doorway of my bedroom. "Good morning, Mae," she said.

I replied, "Good morning, Sister Jason." The formality was something that I would have to get used to.

"Get up, wash up, and dress for your interview with Mr. Loughton. Put on something nice and business like," she said, and then, she turned and left the room.

When I came through the kitchen, I noticed that breakfast was ready, and the table was set.

I went into the bathroom and closed the door. Everything seemed so tight and closed in. I hoped that, in time, I would become adjusted to the small room.

When I came through the kitchen, I braced myself, waiting for the lady to say something.

She did.

"Why did you take so long? Your breakfast will be cold. Now, you'll have to work faster than that if you want to get to work on time every morning," she stated.

I rushed to the bedroom, where I quickly finished dressing, and I was back in the kitchen in a flash. She smiled and motioned for me to be seated in the same place that I had sat in last night. She served our plates and sat across from me.

We ate in silence, and afterwards, she said that she would clear the table, and stated, "Complete your dressing. I'm ready to go out the door."

~~~~~~~~~~~

We made our way to the elevator, as Sister Jason said, "Good Morning," to only the people she knew. She proudly introduced me as her "little girl." She never looked at the others in elevator, and, nor did they recognize our presence. Everyone stood straight and looked forward. We exited the elevator, and the proud looking lady held her head high, and told me to move along and stop staring.

As we made our way down the street, I noticed that Sister Jason was showing clear signs of aging, as she put on her dramatic flair and desperately tried to straighten her slumped shoulders. At seventeen-years-old, even my moderate speed could have left her behind, but she held onto my arm.

We walked over to the avenue to get the downtown bus. On our way, I mailed my letter home. At the bus stop, the lady still held onto me. I looked around, and the thought occurred to me that the city looked so mysterious and dreamy with everybody in a hurry.

Once the bus came, we got on with lots of others. I wasn't used to snuggling up against people whom I didn't know. We rode along, with some getting on and a few getting off. The destination for most was 34th Street.

In no time, we exited the bus near Macy's Department store. The hugeness of the store assailed me. We went inside and found the elevator, and the operator took us to the floor that Sister Jason announced.

We found Mr. Loughton's office, and knocked on the door. We heard him say, "Come in."

We opened the door and walked in. The office was a square room with two desks, each with large leather chairs. One chair was occupied by a brown-haired man, neatly dressed in a dark blue suit.

The man stood while saying, "Good Morning, Nellie." Glancing at me, he stated, "This must be Mae Bloomfield." He extended his hand, and we shook hands simultaneously.

Nellie Jason left the room. Mr. Laughton and I did casual talk. I surmised that he knew quite a bit about me already.

After a short interview, the distinguished looking man told me that I had the job and gave me employment papers to fill out. I was seated at his desk, while he and Nellie stood in the hall, talking like old friends. Sister Jason was so composed and spoke so elegantly, and I did hear her say something about "her little girl." I guessed that the two knew each other quite well.

When I finished the work, I gave him a signal that I had finished.

He politely excused himself and rushed in the room. He glanced over the papers and gave me a nod of approval.

I then handed him my working papers, which, Sister Jason had obtained from The New York State Department of Labor. Of course, I had sent her all of the necessary information.

Mr. Loughton and I left Nellie behind in his office, and we went to observe in my future working area. As we stood waiting for the elevator, we had a good conversation about North Carolina. He had visited the state and had fallen in love with the gorgeous flowers and other greeneries. He had even visited Tryon Palace in New Bern, North Carolina. Loughton had traveled extensively, but he thought that the state of North Carolina was among the most winsome of places. The friendly man seemed saddened by the fact that people, like me, were excluded from its greatness.

I felt so relaxed and comfortable talking with this friendly guy. Mr. Loughton had an excellent ability to make newcomers relax.

We traveled upward, and when we finally stepped out of the elevator, Mr. Loughton explained my future job.

"Mae, you will be working on keyboard machines in the inventory department, and you will be doing keypunching. Right now, we'll go in and meet some of the workers, and then, I'll have Ellen explain your job to you. You'll love the gals in this department. The one from Virginia has the same last name as you do."

I had not forgotten my manners, and said, "Thank you, Mr. Loughlin."

In the department, ladies were working at machineries, using their hands and feet. Cards were going in and after being punched, they came out with holes. Scooping up a few cards, Ellen said, "These holes are for the data-processing system." She then went through the fundamentals, making everything seem simple and easy for me to understand.

Mr. Loughlin asked, "Mae, do you have any questions to ask Ellen?"

Feeling that I was planted in a new world, I answered, "No, I don't."   Excitement engulfed me, as we made our way back to the office.

On our way back, I was told about the worker's union, Macy's Thanksgiving Day Parade, and the twenty percent worker's discount. The best news of all was that Monday morning would be the magic day I would start work.

I was so excited about the future and realized with a sudden certainty that I was really employed. Sister Jason and I left the office to return to the lower floors. She wanted me to look through the ladies clothing. As she went from rack to rack, I just drugged myself behind her with not an inkling of what I wanted. When she realized that I wasn't engaging in the shopping, she started making suggestions.

She then announced, "I want you to throw away that black skirt and buy some new clothes. You don't have to splurge. You just need a few outfits and a winter coat."

Her voice cut at the edge of my heart, *"throw away the black skirt."* I had spent weeks-on- end making my skirt. I dropped my head and swallowed hard, but realized my mouth was dry. Tears rolled down my cheeks.

The lady glanced at me and said, "Let's go home!"

Still holding onto my arm, she headed for the door. I stutter-stepped along, as the tears continued to flow.

When we reached the outside, I started breathing again.

Seemingly, the Sister was trying to find a faster way home, because she stated, "Let's get the subway."

We went around the corner and down some steps. In front of us, the train was coming. We scooted along and reached the doorway. We rushed in with people walking on our heels. Sister Jason found a seat and let me squeeze in beside her.

When we were near 167th Street, we got off. The sun had faded behind the fluffy clouds. We both desired food and rest.

Walking up the stoop, I was told to disregard all of the people who were sitting on the sides.

Once inside, Sister Jason went about her routine, and explained how I was part of the arrangement.

She said, "You are to set the table before the meals, help to cleanup afterward, and please don't put away dishes in a slovenly manner."

I glanced up at the neatly lined shelves with gorgeous dishes and sparkling glassware. The kitchen shelves were neatly lined with paper. The lady made it known that most of the wares were high-quality, and she had inherited them from wealthy people for whom she had once worked.

With a sincere face, the lady stated very clearly, "I am hoping for a better world for you. Go on, attend college, and make something out of yourself."

"I plan to go to college," I said, with even more sincerity.

When night came, my bathroom routine was a bit faster. I said goodnight to my New York mother before going to my room, getting down on my knees and saying an earnest prayer. I sensed that Sister Jason was not going to go easy on me, and I asked the Lord to help me understand her better. I concluded, "Dear Lord. Please help me to be strong enough to stay here and work."

When I got off my knees and got into bed, I was feeling better already. For my mama had always told me that if I really wanted something, just call on the Lord, and He would make a way. My dad had said that God had brought our ancestry out of slavery, and he sure wouldn't leave us now. I had seen and felt the workings of the Lord throughout my life, and I truly believed that things would work out in the city for the good of us all.

~~~~~~~~~~

On Saturday morning, I slept late. I opened my eyes with a throttle, not knowing where I was. Letting my mind sober up, I finally realized that I was in New York City, in Sister Jason's house. Then I knew, I had better get the show on the road.

I straightened up my bed and rushed out to the bathroom. How happy I was to see that she was not in the kitchen; however, the door to her bedroom was open.

As I tried to sneak into the bathroom, she said, in her clear voice, "Good Morning little girl, you had better get yourself together if you plan to go to work on Monday morning. Did you see that clock in your room?"

Standing in the doorway of the bathroom, I answered, "I'll set it for Monday morning."

"You need practice, and I am not going to wake you every morning," she said, while she came closer as if I couldn't hear.

Again, I wished myself back home, but I knew I had to stick it out. I just said, "Yes, Sister Jason," and proceeded to close the door, but kept it cracked so that she could finish.

She then said, "Close the door!"

When I finished in the bathroom, she was in the kitchen. She said, "Your breakfast is on the stove. Let's hope that it's still warm. When you finish eating, clean up, and then we will go to the store to get groceries for next week. Maybe you can pick up something you prefer."

Sister Jason gave me the sweetest smile as I left the room.

I tried my very best to smile, but I probably presented a wry face.

After I finished eating, cleaning, and checking everything in the kitchen, I dressed to go shopping. The lady and I met in the kitchen, and as she took a look around, she announced that I did not put the sugar dish or the salt and pepper shakers in their proper places. She even gave a sigh, as she said, "The sugar dish belongs on the table, and the salt and pepper shakers go on the back of the stove."

I was not going to be defeated. I said slowly and clearly, "I'll put them in their proper places," but was again fighting back tears.

After completing the rearrangement, we went downstairs, out the door, and down the stoop, carrying a rolling cart. I had only ever seen such a cart in a picture prior to this. The sun hid behind the tall buildings, and there were only clouds in the sky. Oh, how I missed the bright sunlight and the singing birds from home.

We walked around the corner and up the street to the food shop. Everyone in the shop knew Sister Jason and spoke to her politely as "Mrs. Jason". She used the telephone at the shop from time to time, and she asked the owner if it would be okay if she sent me to use the telephone. I was introduced as her "little girl from the South, Mae Bloomfield."

There were many people nosing around the butcher's department debating over chicken, veal, lamb, beef, or whatever. I noticed how most of the men in the shop were dressed—high hats and white jackets. The men did not hesitate to give Mrs. Jason the specials she always bought.

I rolled the cart and followed her around as she dropped in items. She did not stop until the two-wheeler was bulging. I wondered about the old lady—by herself—before I came on the scene. How could she lug the two-wheeler up the steps, use keys to get mail and open the doors, and get to her apartment in tact?

Sister Jason pushed herself into the kitchen to put away the meats and vegetables. I tried to help, but I seemed to be in the way.

~~~~~~~~~~~

The city of New York was both exciting and terrifying at the same time, as I looked up at the high-rise buildings. It was Sunday morning. Sister Jason and I were on our way across the street to Elder and Sister Boone's apartment. They were driving us to church.

Sister Jason found a certain mailbox and pushed a button. The buzzer went off, and she pushed the door open. Their apartment was on the first floor. We entered, when someone said, "Come in." I glanced around. The children must have been at play the night before. There were toys, shoes, and clothing thrown around on the floor. I noticed a television was in the living room. Televisions were known as a worldly item; therefore, many of the church members did not own one.

First, the two little girls came out and introduced themselves, and when Elder and Sister came out, they were dressed and ready to go. Just as we were almost out the door, a teenager came out.

The car was full, but we were all comfortably seated when the teen girl was introduced as Jena. She snapped, "Hi," as if she wasn't interested.

I returned the, "Hi."

Sister Jason announced, "This is my little girl from the South."

Jena barely noticed that I was there, and she went on talking about something that had nothing to do with us.

A vexed look came across Sister Jason's face.

I sat in silence all the way to church. I had heard so much about the Church of God, but I had never attended. My mother, along with her sisters and mother, would occasionally attend in New Port News, Virginia.

As we stopped in front of the church, I was surprised. In contrast to the well-known white buildings with a cross on the top, the front resembled most of the storefronts on the block.

When we entered, I was made acquainted with many church folks, who were called "Saints". Then I made my debut down the aisle behind Sister Jason. She stopped at a pew toward the front. I guessed that was her unmarked reserved seat. Letting me in first, she sat on the aisle.

Seemingly, everyone was taking church very seriously. The ladies were wearing hats, gloves, and high-heeled shoes, with purses to match. So was I, with the exception of a hat. Sister Jason had given me a handkerchief to put on my head, until I could buy a hat. As a rule, ladies did not enter the church bareheaded.

The men were dressed in suits, white shirts, ties, and shiny shoes.

Ushers, dressed in white, wandered up and down the aisles, while testimony meeting was in progress. Members stood, one after another, attesting to the goodness of the Lord. They gave witness to living saved, sanctified, and a life above sin. Some recalled the change in their life.

I was mesmerized by the choir. It was the elegant way the members stood with joyful songs ringing throughout the church. The lead singers were twin sisters. One of them played the piano also.

Elder Boone taught the message from the pulpit every Sunday morning, Sunday night, and at Wednesday night prayer meeting. He was a great, calm speaker, who never shouted or screamed, but he did attack sin. On this particular morning, he denounced sexual immorality through the reading of the scriptures. The Deacon stood beside Elder Boone and read from I Corinthians. The Saints of the church brought their own Bibles along so that they could follow the reading of the Word. The Elder spoke with a slight smile on his face, and off his tongue came, "As our Heavenly Bridegroom, God is intent on seeing His children live a chaste and decent life in word and deed."

After morning service, it was clear that Sister Jason was not going to let her little girl get out of her sight. She didn't seem interested in having conversation with others, but she made sure that I met just about everyone. On our way out the door, the lady announced to me, "We'll be getting the bus home. Elder and Sister Boone have an engagement to attend after church."

The lady put her arm through mine, whisked me out the door, and we were on our way, when she whispered, "Elder and Sister Boone shouldn't have taken that Jena into their home. That girl is out of hand."

Of course, I didn't know what to say, but I felt closer to her with her confiding in me. I simply said, "Oh."

She gave me a satisfied look, and then whispered, "I'm surprised at her attending church today."

I gave her a smile to assure her that I understood. It was like having a hen session for the first time.

We got the bus home, knowing full well that we had only a few hours before we would be back at church for the Sunday night service.

We attended the worship service that Sunday night. Sister Jason was completely worn out afterwards. When she returned home, she lost her composure and let on to me that she did not like getting old. Tears welled up in her eyes when she looked in the mirror and spoke about her thinning hair and wrinkled skin.

I didn't know how to cheer her up, so I quietly huddled-up on the corner of the sofa. After all, I had seen a few pictures around her apartment that showed that in her youth she was a raving beauty, and time and age *had* caused a drastic change.

~~~~~~~~~~~

The work week began in the semi-darkness of Monday morning.

As I was on my way to the bathroom, my New York

mother was up cheerfully saying her, "Good Morning!" On the table, I spotted breakfast. A bowl of oatmeal was ready and waiting. Next to my bowl was a brown bag—my lunch!

Later, we walked out the door and down the flight of stairs. She was walking me to the subway entrance. All at once, I felt like—"her little girl". My parents had given me love, but never had I been smothered.

When I reached the bottom of the stairway, I was overwhelmed to see such an array of people. Sister Jason had warned me that there would be more of a crowd on Monday morning, but I had not expected a multitude.

The train stopped, and the door opened. I was in the middle of the mass of humanity who pushed through the door, carrying me inside. Standing in the crowd, I realized that New York was not a piece of cake, but just maybe, - an improvement over the South.

I shuddered at the thought of mistakenly getting off the train someplace other than 34th Street. Seeing through the crowd was impossible, so I kept my ears to the ground.

When the train stopped at 34th, I got off as fast as the crowd would allow me. I rushed in the door of Macy's Department Store, into the elevator, and was let off on the floor of the inventory department.

Seemingly, everyone was waiting for me—the new girl, who would join them in the inventory department. I suppose becoming a keypuncher was a natural thing for someone who had been so involved in typing in her high school days, but still some uncertainty crept over me. As I entered the room, Ellen came toward me with a pleasant smile on her face. She was tall and slender, and I thought of her as beautiful. Lips paused in a soft voice, she gave me additional directions and information.

I gave her my full attention, and I was surprisingly titillated by all the possibilities that awaited me at Macy's Department Store. Later in the morning, we were a team that was touching, tapping and punching on the machines.

The morning zipped by, and everyone was ready for lunch.

Some of the people went out to eat, including Ellen, and others were brown bagging it. Within my bag was a baloney sandwich that was neatly wrapped in wax paper. The lettuce, tomato, cheese, and pickles were in separate wrappers. I think that was the best lunch that I had ever eaten.

Millie asked, "Where are you from?"

Speaking the way Sister Jason asked me to speak, I said, "I am from New Bern, North Carolina."

"Now, where exactly is that located?"

"In the eastern part of North Carolina, near the Atlantic Ocean," I proudly announced.

Millie Bloomfield thought we might be relatives and expressed her surprise, as she said, "I am from Danville, Virginia and lived near the North Carolina state line." Her smile gave way to dimples on her beautiful dark brown skin. She was nothing short of a beauty.

Susan, the blonde, was drinking a Pepsi Cola, and mistakenly burped. Lips pursed in a whisper, she said, "Please excuse me." However, all of us found that what she had done was amusing. How could we resist laughing?

Then there was Patty, who was thinking naughtily, cleared her throat, and gave us some good humor.

We enjoyed listening to each other, and we returned to our work energized.

At the end of the day, there was no doubt that I liked my job. My new world was stretching out before me, and all seemed pleasing.

When I reached home in the evening, Sister Jason was standing on the stoop waiting for me. A smile was lurking in her eyes, and as I drew closer, it spread to the rest of her face. She didn't exactly give me a hug, but instead, she put her hand on my shoulder as we went through the doorway. I could tell that she was happy to have me as her little girl.

When we walked through the door, the delightful smell of food permeated the kitchen. I readied myself for dinner. While eating, we discussed my job. The evening meals consisted of meat, two vegetables, bread, and a dessert with tea or lemonade. So far, I had relished all of the meals.

The partnership of cleaning the kitchen gave us a few hours before bedtime. My New York mother expressed her desire that I read *The New York Times*. She glanced at my expression, and said, "You must know that an educated person should be up-to-date on current events. After all, we don't own a TV, and most of the Saints don't own one."

My fleeting impression about the gigantic paper on the table by the sofa wasn't the greatest. However, I was aware that her suggestion was a very extraordinary idea.

In my New York mother's eyes, curling up on the sofa was a sloppy, slouchy way to sit. She expressed her disdain towards people who signified laziness or incompetence, and procrastination was out of the question.

I went to a corner of the couch, sat straight with my spine against the back and felt considerably comfortable, while my saintly mother sat on the opposite end with her big round magnifying glasses. As I read, I realized that reading the *New York Times* was among the most informative things that I had ever done. I was graciously informed before I came to the most eye-catching articles that we had discussed in high school. I read: **"Brown v. Board of Education**: The U.S. Supreme Court issued its historic *Brown v. Board of Education*, 347 U.S. 483, on May 17, 1954. The decision declared all laws establishing segregated schools to be unconstitutional, and it called for the desegregation of all schools throughout the nation."

Below that article, I read on: **"Arkansas National Guard and the integration of Central High School:** Several segregationists councils threatened to hold protests at Central High and physically block the black students from entering the school. Governor Orval Faubus deployed the Arkansas National Guard to support the segregationists. The sight of a line of soldiers blocking out the students made national headlines and polarized the nation on this day, September 4,

1957."

My eyes drifted away from the page, and I took in a breath of fresh air. The news about the mean-spirited people cast a gloom within my heart. I became cognizant of the fact that someday I must return to North Carolina. It was incumbent upon me that I help with the fight for civil rights.

Sister Jason sat peering at me over her glasses and asked, "Are you alright, Mae?"

"Oh yes!" I said.

"That must be a hard pill to swallow," the lady stated.

She seemingly thought the worst about the people from the South, and I wasn't going to feed her thoughts. So, I just said, "Yes, it is."

I went back to my reading. One of the nine students, Elizabeth Eckford, said:

They moved closer and closer . . .Somebody started yelling . . . I tried to see a friendly face somewhere in the crowd, someone who maybe could help. I looked into the face of an old woman and it seemed to be a kind face, but when I looked at her again, she spat on me.

10 CHAPTER TEN

MAE

"...there was—and always had been . . . a tradition

based on the simple idea that we have

a stake in one another, and that what

binds us together is greater than what drives us apart,

and that if enough people believe in the truth of that

proposition

and act on it, then we might not solve every problem,

but we can get something done."

~ President Barack Obama

My first work week was fine and dandy, and another Sunday was upon us. We did attend prayer meeting on Wednesday night, but Sunday, the first day of the week, was our Sabbath, and of course, Sister Jason wouldn't have thought of missing the service.

This Sunday, Elder Boone had a car full of relatives; so, we went for the bus. Sister Jason put her street face on and expected me to do the same. She looked straight ahead as we stopped for the light to change. We crossed the street and went right for the bus.

When we reached the church, the youth group was coming out of Sunday school. Sister Jason passed the group with her eyes focused ahead. I noticed a handsome young man. Our eyes met, and he smiled at me. I returned the smile.

Sister Jason noticed. She took my arm and ushered me down the aisle, saying, "I don't want you with that group. Not with that—Sister Little."

On that same Sunday, I joined the Church of God. Sister Jason was pleased that I was governed by the "Holy Spirit" and had become a part of the church. She even gave me money to put into the collection basket. When I dropped my envelope into the basket. I could tell that the Lady felt as I did—that I had faith and trust in the Lord.

Elder Boone spoke in a gentle voice as he prayed and received me into the house of God. Happiness and Holiness were shining in his eyes.

After church service, the Saints' faces glowed with peace and happiness as they welcomed me into the Church of God. With love and handshakes, they gladly received me. I felt that we were together in spirit, as my heart beat with the rhythm of the Holy Spirit.

Sister Jason waited patiently for an opportunity to get me out the door. She was completely satisfied when we were swaying together as we walked toward the bus stop.

When we reached the apartment, we had dinner. Sister Jason suggested that we not go back to Church on Sunday nights. She looked tired as she said, "You need your rest to return to work on Monday mornings."

As I went for pencil and paper, I stated, "I will write to my family, and then, I will read the *New York Times*."

Looking pleasantly pleased, she went about her business.

When I was done with my letter to my family, I picked up the paper dated September 9, 1957. Little Rock, Arkansas School District was still making headlines. The school system issued a statement condemning the governor's deployment of soldiers to the school.

The next week flew by, and Friday was payday. As we left work, we stopped by the office to pick up our checks. I put the envelope in my pocketbook and clenched it all the way home.

Later, we went to the bank to cash my check. Sister Jason did not trust banks, so we had a special place in the house to save the money.

I sent a tiny percentage of my money home, and I was struck by a surprise statement from the lady: "Give a percentage to the church."

My first notion was, *"I don't want to give any to the church,"* but I instantly remembered that I was taught that one should give a tenth of his earnings to the church. It was shown to me right there in the scriptures. So, I agreed on a percentage; however, I knew I had no other choice anyway.

On the following Saturday, I assisted with the cleaning and dusting of the apartment. When I finished dusting the floor, I opened the window and shook the mop out the window. After closing the window, I turned and observed my impeccable job. That's when we heard a knock on the door.

Sister Jason rushed from her bedroom and went for the door. As she looked through the peephole, she asked, "Who is it?"

The voice from the other side of the door said, "The policeman."

She opened the door, while I stood with the mop in my hand.

The policeman glanced at me and asked, "Did someone in this apartment shake a mop out the window?"

Both people eyed me, so I decided to move out of sight and ditch the mop.

While standing out of the field of vision, I could tell that my New York mother and the policeman's discussion was a conflict of interest.

Sister Jason explained, "She's just a little girl from the

South, and didn't know that she wasn't supposed to shake the mop out the window."

The policeman asked, "Didn't she see all the clothes hanging under the window?"

"Evidently she didn't. If she knew, she wouldn't have done it."

"Well, whether she knew better or not, she did it, and she has committed a misdemeanor."

"Couldn't you just forget it this time and give her another chance?"

"No, she should have seen the clothes on the clothesline beneath her."

"My poor child didn't know any better."

"I am going to write her a citation, and she will have to appear in court."

There was silence, and I could envision his writing the citation. Then I heard the door open, and the policeman saying, "Have a good day." I did not hear an answer. The door closed.

I waited. Sister Jason came into view. Her eyes looked heavy, and her mouth was pinched with anger. She looked at me and said, "I just don't understand why he couldn't just give you a warning."

All of a sudden, I realized that she was angry with the policeman— not me.

She, then, squinted her eyes and asked, "Did you ever look out the window?"

"Yes—I—did," I reluctantly answered.

"And you didn't see the multiple lines of laundry flapping in the breeze?" Sister Jason questioned me.

"I saw them, but—a-a-ah, but I didn't remember them," I said pitifully."

Well, anyway, we're in this together," she said without asking any more questions.

At that moment, I really knew that I was her little girl. I could tell that she loved me as one of her very own.

Sister Jason had said very little about her daughter, who

lived in nearby New Jersey. From time to time, she would make remarks such as: "I would love to have Flo attend church with me. Flo wants to have everything her way. My daughter is a strong woman." She did say that her son drowned as a pre-teen. So far, she didn't seem able or willing to discuss it with me.

After dinner on that Saturday night, we relaxed and caught up on the news. We had picked up the newspaper and a choice of magazine from the newsstand. The magazine carried an article on the Delany sisters who hailed from Raleigh, North Carolina. I was aware that they had joined the great wave of black Americans who headed north in search of opportunities.

Bessie Delany found that even New York was not the promised land as one thought. There were many jobs that had not opened up to the blacks, even in New York. She had become only the second black woman licensed to practice dentistry in the city. Her sister, Sadie, was the first black ever to teach domestic science on the high school level in the New York City Public Schools.

The composition told about the sisters living in Harlem, getting acquainted with legendary figures, such as Cab Calloway. Cab was associated with the Cotton Club and had begun to play roles in stage productions.

Reading the article about the ladies from Raleigh, North Carolina made me feel just a little homesick. I returned to my bedroom for the night, as I recalled a note that was given to me the last day of high school. I had pushed it in the side of my bag before leaving home. I pulled it out and read it. It said:

Hi Mae,

. . . I will be spending some time in Teaneck, New Jersey at this address ... Please get in touch with me.

Love,

Bill

In the quiet of the night, I became both anxious and embarrassed at my notion to write to the boy whom I had enjoyed knowing so much in the last months of my high school days. I struggled to find words, but later mustered the courage to write.

Hi Bill,

I am now in New York City. I am working at Macy's Department Store on 34th Street. Please meet me on Wednesday, September 13th at four o'clock, near the elevators. I will have one hour to spend with you.

Love,

Mae

I yawned as I reread my letter. After folding and sliding it into the envelope, I licked the seal and reluctantly placed one of my three cent stamps onto it.

The next few days before that Wednesday, I felt apprehensive, but excited. The whole world was spinning around me. It was quite difficult to concentrate on my reading of the newspaper, but I did manage to read about the citywide prayer service that was called in Little Rock, Arkansas the day before, September 12, 1957. The article went on to say that, "Even President Dwight Eisenhower attempted to de-escalate the situation by summoning Governor Orval Faubus for a meeting, warning him not to defy the Supreme Court's ruling."

~~~~~~~~~~

On the night before that particular Wednesday, there were hours between waking and drifting through nonsensical dreams. My nervous mind ran through the fast-approaching day of meeting Bill by the elevator. I awoke early in the morning. Somehow, I managed to ready myself for work, eat breakfast, and get out of the apartment.

The first hint of cold weather was in the air. I shivered as questions simmered in the back of my mind. Questions such as, "Did Sister Jason question my actions this morning? Was I being dishonest or underhanded?" and most importantly, "Would she find out?"

At my workplace, the girls talked about stuff—boyfriends, dating, partying, movies, and much more. Of course, they politely invited me to join them, but I knew that it was out of the question. My lame excuses were fit for a laugh, so I didn't bother to observe their faces when I gave my reason for not joining them. Many times, my answers would echo back at me, but I just brushed the mimics off, and felt that time would take care of itself. As usual, I quietly worked the day away.

In the afternoon, I stood by the elevator on the first floor. My fright, already enormous, grew even greater as time passed. Just as I was about to change my mind, I saw Bill wading his way through the crowd, coming in my direction.

When we stood face to face, I didn't know if we were to hug or shake hands. After standing and staring at each other for minutes, he took me by my hand, and we made our way toward the door.

Out on 34th Street, an ominous breeze swept over us and the rain fell softly upon our heads. We were a seventeen-year-old and an eighteen-year-old, both full of life and enjoying our stroll on the streets of New York City. Walking past the windows, seeing our reflections, tickled us to no end.

When the giggling cooled down, we held hands and ran through the streets, going no place in particular. With our fingers intertwined, I felt as wonderful as I did when we were in high school. We felt like young lovers gone wild between the tall buildings on some street we did not recognize. Turning at corners and walking straight ahead, we found a place to buy food. We went into a café and found a booth. Our conversation was nil as we sat looking into each other's eyes.

Ice cream was our choice of food. Bill was so funny when he made a mustache with his vanilla ice cream. We just couldn't stop laughing. When the waitress arrived, each of us pulled out change until we had enough to pay.

We were feeling perfectly content as we left the cafe to continue our stroll. Suddenly, I looked at my watch—five-thirty! "Sister Jason is probably waiting for me," I said aloud, while jerking my hand away from him. I raced through the streets, going around and between the people. Bill was screaming,

"Wait for me!"

The streets rose up to meet me, and the wind was at my back, as I made my way down one street and then the other, until I was on 34thStreet. I ran down 34th Street until I did not recognize my surroundings. It dawned on me that I was going the wrong way. I quickly turned around on my heels and sped off in the other direction.

When I was almost at the familiar terminal, the crowd thickened, and impeded my progress. After ducking and dodging around people, I got my first chance, and scooted down into the subway. When I entered the train car, I took a deep breath. My nervousness would not allow me to sit, so I stood squeezing the post with my thoughts on Bill. I had not said goodbye to him. I wondered what he felt about me now. The ride home seemed longer than ever.

At my destination, I quickened my steps off the train, ran through the terminal, and up the steps - into the streets. I felt suddenly frightened. From a distance, I could see Sister Jason standing on the stoop with a piece of paper in her hand. It resembled a letter.

As I drew closer, I noticed that her face was racked with stress and little lines appeared around her eyes. She tightened her lips and asked, "Where on God's green earth have you been?"

I attempted to reply, but nothing came out—just a gasp.

She shook the letter at me, and said, "You've been somewhere with this boy, haven't you? It says right here on this letter—that he would meet you by the elevator."

I was shocked. I blinked, suddenly feeling on the spot.

Everyone on the stoop sat quietly, staring up at us.

My eye threatened tears, and I felt awful.

She put her chin up, and said, "Let's go inside."

I followed her as she pushed the door open for me and let the door slam behind us.

When we reached the inside of the apartment, she took a deep breath, and said, "Sit down! We'll have to get to the bottom of this!"

While pressing hard upon my frail thoughts to find the correct way to explain the ordeal, I slowly sank onto the couch, as tears rolled down my face. I could feel her eyes on me. I knew she wanted to shake me and make me talk.

I sucked in air until my lungs were full, as I looked at Sister Jason. She was hovering over me. She was watching me closely—wanting me to say something.

I wanted to come right out and tell her the truth—about how lonely I had become without any association with the youth. After all, I had had a so-called boyfriend since first grade. Being without a friend my age, made me sad. When I reached my teens, and was a high schooler, I had the time of my life. Quite often, I found fresh love and held hands, while my tummy swiveled. Oh! How I missed that kind of life. However, I felt incapable when it came to explaining my feelings to Sister Jason. But I wasn't going to lie. I was taught that lying would send you straight to hell. No detours. No second chances. Straight into the fiery pit where Satan was waiting with his pitch fork to turn you over when you were done on one side.

I remembered how my brother, Robert, had gotten the worse whipping of his life when he had lied. I had told on him and got him into a world of trouble. Mama was determined to get the truth out of him. She said, "I am going to whip you until you tell me the truth."

I felt pity for him and cried, "Just tell the truth, Robert—just say that you did it, even if you didn't.

Robert cried out, "I did it, Mama—I smoked!"

Mama quit and said, "Just tell me the truth."

Everything was quiet. I looked up and the lady was staring at me. She was still mad, I guess because I was silent. My mother didn't allow me to talk back.

Sister Jason then asked, "What is your problem?"

I answered, "I don't have one."

Her eyes looked glazed over, "Yes you do. You went somewhere, and I don't know where, with this boy, man or whatever." After waiting for a while, I could see her growing frustrations, as she said, "Mae, let's—just eat—our dinner."

Slowly I stood, gathered my belongings, and took them to my bedroom. I stood in the room, while feeling an ache to be somewhere else other than this apartment in New York.

When I thought that it was time for me come out, I crept out and quietly went through the kitchen to visit the bathroom. I stayed in there as long as I possibly could.

When I came out of the bathroom, as always, my colorful plate sat waiting for me with meat, vegetables, fruits, and bread. Sister Jason always took great pains to give me a balanced diet. She said the blessing. As we ate, a long, awkward silence yawned between us, and I could hear the ticking of the clock. I didn't know what to say. I wanted to tell her all about our laughter and stroll down the streets of New York City, but it seemed so childish- or maybe, foolish.

My chin went up, the lady craned her neck to hear, but my defensive mechanism jelled, and suddenly tears filled my eyes again.

After eating, we always did the dishes together. She filled the sink with water, while I silently cleared the table. We worked in quietness. I really couldn't think of how I could tell her about our little meander without sounding silly.

When the kitchen was finished, we did our customary relaxing: reading, writing or the like. Sister Jason started her saintly talk again. She said, "You know, that boy could ruin your life. You fall for his lies and the next thing you know, you'll be pregnant. You say you want to go to college. Then, you'll never get to college."

That mildly got my attention. I did want so badly to go off to college. It was my dream to become a teacher like Mrs. Rouse. I said, "We just walked the streets together."

She stood over me. Her eyes flashed sadness and anger. She looked older than she really was. Her voice was escalating again. "I can't believe you! I can't believe you would walk around the streets while I'm here worrying about where you are. You want me to send you back down South to your mother?"

I had trouble breathing, but my only answer was, "No." I was hoping she would calm down. After all, I was not a criminal. I had done nothing wrong. We had just had fun, and that was what I was longing for.

She lost her composure. "Where did you go?"

"We walked down 34th Street, turned after about three blocks, went a couple more, turned, and found a food station. We ordered ice cream, and the time passed away—really fast," I said, very meekly.

The lady didn't say anything for a few minutes. When she did speak, she was again the calm, dignified lady that I once knew. She said, "Mae, if you don't know it, I'm responsible for you. I asked you to come here. You are under age. Remember, you even had to get working papers to enable you to work." She narrowed her eyes, took in a breath of air, and asked, "Do you understand me so far?

"Yes, I do," I said calmly.

Tenderly and in a straightforward fashion, she said, "Just let me know if you are going to be late, and for God's sake, let me know where and who you are going with." Still glaring, she asked, "Do you know you were not acting responsibly?"

Still struggling for words, my jaw muscles clenched and unclenched.

Sister Jason shook her head in disgust.

I knew that I was at a point where I had to say something. I wanted so much to explain, but I just said, "Yes, I guess I'm not."

The tall lady shadowed over me, waiting for more. Not a sound could be heard except for the clock ticking away on the wall.

Finally, I came to the conclusion that she was going to wait me out. I cleared my throat and finally said, "I'm sorry I caused you to worry."

A smile flicked across Sister Jason's face. She reiterated what she had said when I first arrived, "If you need to call home, remember you have Elder & Sister Boone's telephone number. They are helping to look out for you. Do you always have the number with you?"

"Yes, I have it in my bag," I said, trying to sound *real—real* responsible.

11 CHAPTER ELEVEN

MAE

"You can learn more about

human nature by reading the Bible

than by living in New York."

~ William Lyon Phelps

One night later on, we read and discuss the Church of God's Sunday school lesson. However, we didn't attend Sunday school, and I didn't own a Bible. Sister Jason announced that she would take me to Mr. Louis Copeland's bookstore to buy a Bible. Louis, who was the brother of the founder of the Church of God, was well known and owned a store on 125th and 7th Avenue. He prided himself on having or being able to get a copy of any book written by a black author since 1900.

When we were finished with our Bible lesson, I scanned the newspaper. One of the headlines was **"Armed Escort."** The paper reported that "Woodrow Wilson Mann, the mayor of Little Rock, asked President Eisenhower to send federal troops to enforce integration and protect the nine students. On September 24th, 1957, the President ordered the 101st Airborne Division of the United States Army—without its black soldiers, who could rejoin the division later—to Little Rock and federalized the entire 10,000-member Arkansas National Guard, taking it out of the hands of Faubus."

The following Saturday, I embraced the opportunity to visit the bookstore. Once again, my New York mother hung onto me as we walked toward the subway. Even on Saturday, a horde of people filled the train car, going someplace or somewhere.

Before a certain stop, Sister Jason got up and stood by the door. I followed her off of the train and up the subway, and behold, I was in a different world. As we walked the streets, Sister Jason held onto my arm as she spoke, "This is the urban ghetto."

While this part of the city was terrifying, I was grateful to learn a new word, I repeated, "Ghetto."

"We'll talk about this later, but I do want you to know that the largest percent of these people once lived in rural areas in the South."

The lady clung to my arm, and I could feel her weight on my shoulder as we walked the streets. She drew my attention to the grungy section of New York City, and wanted me to see the urban poor—the urban Negros and how they were ill-housed. She vehemently warned me that I should never venture into that area alone.

After the grueling hike, we went to visit the bookstore. Mr. Louis Copeland greeted us at the door. Sister Jason introduce me as "Mae Bloomfield." With drooping jaws, she went straight for a chair, slinking down onto it and taking a deep breath. She was truly exhausted from all of the walking.

My eyes scanned the remarkable room of books. Mr. Copeland joined me and introduced me to several authors, including Langston Hughes, whose first book was *The Weary Blues*, published in 1926 by the Urban League Magazine. Langston's book, *Not Without Laughter*, was published by Random House in 1930. Mr. Copeland also showed me some of James Baldwin's books, like, *Go Tell It on the Mountain*, published in 1953 by Knopf, and *Giovanni's Room*, published by Dial Press, N.Y in 1956.

The bookstore held many notable works of James Weldon Johnson. As I held some of his books, I was reminded of the song that we had sung so often back in school, "Lift Ev'ry Voice and Sing." James wrote the poem in 1899, and soon after, his brother, Rosamond, set it to music. It became known as the "Negro National Anthem," a title that the NAACP adopted and promoted.

In my brown arms, I cradled the book, *Paul Robeson, Negro*. I had heard so much about Robeson while in high school. As I thumbed through the pages, I noticed that it was written by his wife, Eslanda Goode Robeson, published in 1930, by Harper & Brothers.

As I placed the Robeson book back on the shelf, my eyes caught sight of a book entitled, *The Ghetto*. I opened it and read a few pages: "The black ghetto in America is essentially a Northern urban invention in cities such as New York, Chicago, Los Angeles, Detroit, Philadelphia, Washington, DC, St Louis, Baltimore, Cleveland, Houston and New Orleans." Thumbing through, I read here and there, "The urban ghetto seemed to have had little contact with whites. They, who live in the ghetto, seemed to have little say-so about community affairs. Around the dark ghetto is an invisible wall."

I had never visited a bookstore or library, and I was greatly impressed about what was housed under its roof. I walked around, looked around, and read covers that had the names of influential African Americans on them whom we had studied and discussed in the North Carolina Public School System: *W.E.B. Du Bois and Civil Rights, Harriett Tubman, A Humanitarian, The Dred Scott Case,* and on and on. But in the end, I only bought the Bible that Sister Jason had instructed me to buy beforehand. I sensed that she felt that it would not be expedient of me to spend my college money.

On the way home, Sister Jason picked up a magazine. Louis had told us about Claude Brown, who grew up in a tenement on 146th Street and 8th Avenue, and he was now in the process of writing a book, and in the meantime, Brown was writing magazine articles.

My stomach was growling by the time we reached our

street. Sister Jason spoke of her hunger as she stood slightly humped, while pulling herself up the steps to our apartment.

Once inside, Sister Jason seemed very tired and crabby. Again, she mentioned her younger days when she was so vibrant and energetic. She could not understand her downward spiral, and she was absolutely shrieking about yesteryears. The lady was bringing up the same old sad story once again.

Tiptoeing around, helping her to prepare the food, I didn't respond, fearing that I would say the wrong thing. Furthermore, there was absolutely nothing I could do about it.

As we sat down to eat, silence crept in around us. We sat munching on our chicken salad sandwiches garnished with lettuce, sliced tomatoes, and pickles. As we quenched our thirst, I could hear the gulping of the lemonade and the ticking of the clock.

Later that night, we read Claude Brown's article in the magazine. He wrote about the Southern blacks seeking opportunities in Northern cities. He said, "Going to New York was goodbye to the cotton fields, goodbye to 'Massa Charlie,' goodbye to the chain gang, and, most of all, goodbye to those sunup-to-sundown working hours. One no longer had to wait to get to heaven to lay his burden down; burdens could be laid down in New York. Yet, life in the promised land of New York turned out to be much harder than the migrants had imagined."

~~~~~~~~~~

Sister Jason seemed to have great plans for me. She graciously announced that we would be visiting Radio City Music Hall as soon as she could make reservations.

The corner of my mouth curled, and I stopped dead in my tracks. I wanted to ask, "Do the Saints go to those places?" We had been taught that dancing was a sin, and one should not participate or be entertained by it. However, becoming a professional dancer was my secret passion, and I truly felt that I possessed innate skills. Going to see the Rockettes would be a dream come true. In fact, I had secretively read about the many shows in the city, but never dreamed of actually attending.

I truly loved working at Macy's. I became completely entrenched in my job, and I had forgotten the mop-shaking incident. When the letter arrived summoning me to court a few days later, I was snatched back to reality. It was obvious that I would have to miss a few hours of work.

The night before the court appearance, Sister Jason gave me her stern say, "Please speak up in court tomorrow, sit up straight, and please, no crying."

I wanted to reason with her and tell her how automatic my tears were, but I seriously doubted that she would understand. So, once again, I tucked my tail and took to a path of timidity.

My mind was racing a mile a minute, and I found it impossible to read the magazines and newspapers. I just wanted to be alone to think about the next day. I said, "Goodnight," in the most pleasant tone that I could muster.

She answered, "Goodnight, dear."

I knew that I had to find something to wear to court. I couldn't conceive of how one would dress for a stay of execution.

Going to the closet to get something to wear, I became blinded by tears. My hands were shaking, and my knees were knocking.

I knew that I needed to calm down and find some sense of humor in the scenario.

Moving back and forth from the closet to the bed, mixing and matching, I came up with a comfortable outfit with a cheery color.

Later, I lay in bed looking up at the ceiling. The happenings for the coming day pressed in on my frail thoughts. Again, I listened to the city noises. Sometime between 12:00 and 1:00 in the morning, I fell off to sleep.

The following morning, I didn't want to get out of bed or see Sister Jason. I slowly sat up, and then eased out of bed, tiptoeing around the room while I made up the bed.

After dressing and getting ready, I entered the kitchen, where Sister Jason was getting breakfast ready. She did her usual morning greeting. The Lady was humming a happy song. I even glanced at her face. She seemed unconcerned about our coming day. I thought, "Maybe, she has been to court and found that there was nothing to it."

Sister Jason's demeanor relieved me of some of my worries.

Out on the busy city streets, under the still gray sky, we hopped from bus to bus until we reached the courthouse.

As we stepped off the bus, we stood in front of a vast building with numerous steps. Staring at the steps, Sister Jason's shoulders dropped a few inches. Later, we mustered the courage to begin the climb. After we began our ascension, we took an occasional breather. When we reached the top, Sister Jason was breathing hard. She put her head down and leaned against the wall. When she was feeling better, we stood and looked around. Gray clouds were floating overhead, and the sun was trying to peek through. Our skirts flapped in the breeze.

We found our way to the lobby. A gentleman guided us to the proper room.

Since I had never been in a courthouse, the courtroom epitomized everything I felt that the room would look like. It looked remarkable with its plush runner up the aisle. Long, mahogany benches with a few nicks in them filled the room on both sides of the runner. Historical pictures hung on the walls. The room looked pleasant enough.

People sat in different spots, while their voices traveled across the room. I followed Sister Jason, and we found a seat near the front of the room. Just as I was sitting down, I looked up, and a man entered from a door in front of us. He sat down in a chair, in what resembled a pulpit. I looked at him in profile and saw a short, stubby man in a gray suit. He had a red face with thick glasses stuck on his nose. He purposely rose and unbuttoned his jacket as his eyes scanned the audience.

Sister Jason whispered, "He is the presiding judge."

I gave her a nod that said okay.

The judge hit his gavel and said, "Court is in order!"

The first person that was called was a lady by the name of Sally Callio. She stood before the judge and he said, "You are charged with not removing your canine waste from the streets." He paused and went on to read the City Pet Law. "The canine waste law here in New York states that it shall be the duty of each dog owner or person having possession, custody, or control of a dog to remove any feces left by his or her dog on any sidewalk, gutter, street, or other public area."

The lady attempted to explain her side of the story.

The judge asked if she was guilty of the act, or not guilty.

She attempted to explain again, without giving a direct answer.

The judge certainly had no sense of humor as he announced, "Guilty as charged!" and then hit the gavel.

Ms. Callio moved toward her seat as she bit her lower lip and carried mist in her eyes.

Several other misdemeanors were in order. I was beginning to think that mine had been forgotten or forgiven when I was deafened by the call: "Mae Bloomfield!"

As I rose from my seat, I felt that the court had formulated an evil plan of revenge against me. I stood before the magistrate with my feet together as if I were going to demonstrate a ballet. My lips trembled. I was definitely scared.

The judge sipped from his glass of water and then sniffed with indignation. His voice howled around my head when he stated my case and gave me my charges.

I watched his fat hands as he waved them across the desk. His hands retreated, raising his gavel and pronouncing me – "Guilty."

I stood and fastened my jaws tight to keep my chin from quivering. When I began to move away, I turned back and raised my brows in question, but then it struck me that there was no way I could weasel out of being guilty. Exhaling, I went to find my seat.

Sister Jason put her arm around me and whispered, "Are

you alright?"

Trying hard to keep my voice low, I answered, "I think so."

Turning her face my way again, she said, "We don't have to stay any longer. Let's go."

We softly walked to the door. I avoided all eyes by looking past them.

Following behind Sister Jason, we found our way out of the building. The clouds were still hanging low over the city, but at least there was no rain. We stood on the top steps and breathed in the air.

After lingering for minutes, the lady caught on to my arm, and we gently moved downward.

When we were on the street, we found the bus stop, and only had a few minutes' wait. In mid-day, the bus was not crowded, so we had a choice of seats. We took the front seats. I enjoyed the view, while, I guessed that Sister Jason was getting some rest. Contrary to the fact that I was charged as guilty, I was feeling a great sense of relief.

Somewhere about midpoint of our return trip, Sister Jason and I went our separate ways. I would finish my day at work and she would return home.

Everyone at work welcomed me at midday, and I was delighted to be there, with a clear mind.

After the workday was over, I walked to the subway and rode home, feeling a sense of deliverance. With that emotion, I strolled to the apartment. Sister Jason was not waiting for me on the stoop.

My heart leaped and my stomach fluttered, as I thought that something might have happen to the lady. I raced up the steps, flung open the outside door, and took two steps at a time to the second floor. I had trouble finding my key. It had only been used a few times. While I was fingering around in my bag, the door flung open. Sister Jason stood in the doorway with a frown on her face. She asked, "Was something or somebody after you?"

With glaring eyes, I said, "No-o-o, but I didn't see you on

the stoop, and I—I—thought—ah—ah—maybe . . .

The lady cracked a smile and said, "I was late getting home. I had to get our dinner together."

I finally exhaled, and then inhaled the spicy aroma. The kitchen was smelling absolutely divine.

Dinner was pork roast with a brown gravy, rice, a green salad, and spiced apple pie for our dessert.

After cleaning up the kitchen together, we sat down to read. That night, on September 29, 1957, I selected to read the entertainment section first. Scanning through the rest of the paper, I was determined to stay abreast of the Little Rock ordeal. The topic was in bold print: **"Little Rock Central High Under Protection."** I read, "The Arkansas National Guard joined the 101st Airborne Division, but the nine students were still subjected to being spat on and called names by the white students. Melba Pattillo had acid thrown in her eyes. Minnijean Brown said that they were told that they would have to take a lot and were warned not to fight back."

~~~~~~~~~~

On a chilly Sunday morning in October, we were able to get a ride to church with Elder and Sister Boone. The talk was all about the trip to Washington, D.C. for the baptism. I was to be one of the new members that would participate in the ceremony. It was said that Sister Little would be taking the Youth Group, but I was fully aware that I would not be joining them.

When we reached church, we sat in our same seats and listened to the testimonies, sermon, and songs. As I was busy getting the sermon in shorthand, I thought about my mother, and how much she must have been enjoying the sermons that I had been typing out and sending home to her.   This particular Sunday, Elder Boone preached from the book of Proverbs. Standing by the Elder, a Deacon read the verses from the Bible, "Fret not yourself because of evildoers, and be not envious of the wicked; for the evil man has no future; the lamp of the wicked will be put out." Elder Boone repeated, "Fret not yourself because of evildoers." He went on to say that, "Worrying about evildoers is undue worry. Evildoers are those who have an appreciation for sin and will encourage others to do the same. They would bring with them destruction and devastation."

The members found the scriptures, were reading along, waving their hands and saying, "Amen!"

After service, once again, my New York mother was not in the mood for small talk with the church members. She held me by the arm and we went straight for the bus.

The thoughts that came to my mind were the same ones that I formed the first Sunday that I visited church. The recollection was, "Sister Jason was a woman that didn't trust easily. Her relationship with many of the church members was not healthy."

When we reached our apartment, we warmed our Sunday supper that was cooked the day before. We discussed our upcoming trip to Radio City Music Hall, which was coming up in the latter part of the week. Sister Jason had the tickets in her hand.

Later, when we were sitting calmly and eating our Sunday dinner, Sister Jason made an announcement. I gasped and almost choked on my food when Sister Jason said that we were going to Yankee Stadium to see and hear Billy Graham. I knew that he was from North Carolina, and I thought of him as another white Southerner.

My Northern mother had a great deal of respect for him. She tried to explain away all of my preconceived ideas about the minister. Regardless, I was always ready to participate in any event that she suggested. Going to functions with her got me out into the city, and also softened my caged-bird feeling.

12 CHAPTER TWELVE

MAE

If you're walking down

the right path and

you'll willing to keep walking,

eventually you'll make progress.

~ Barack Obama

Sister Jason was definitely a Radio City Music Hall insider. When we talked about our trip, it soon became obvious that she had special knowledge about the place. I couldn't have been more excited about our night out. We dressed in our finest for the occasion. Sister Jason said she preferred to take the bus rather than the subway; she felt that by taking the bus she wouldn't have as many steps to climb or have as far to walk.

Just standing under the bright lights in front of Radio City Music Hall was much to behold. We walked inside, and I gasped. It was inconceivable. Our tickets were collected, and we followed behind the usher as he escorted us to our seats.

After we were seated, Sister Jason whispered, "I hope you enjoy this. We were able to get great seats."

I whispered back, "This is great. I think I'm going to love it."

The Rockettes were spectacular in their costumes. I was

mesmerized by the back bending and leg kicking. They sure wowed the audience. The show was all that I had expected and more.

When the magic world with all of its enchantment ended, we left for the bus stop.

Riding home on the bus, I realized that I was getting used to the bright lights and big city. I was loving all that it had to offer.

We entered our apartment. Sister Jason went straight to her bedroom, and I went to mine. A few minutes later, we heard the ring of our buzzer.

Sister Jason rush from her room and pushed the inside button, asking, "Who is it?"

A voice came through that answered, "Elder Boone! Just wanted to give you a telephone message—Flo said that she would be coming tomorrow."

"Uh-huh," the Lady stammered.

"Did you hear me?" Elder Boone asked, in his very loud, clear voice.

"Oh yes. Thank you!" She hurriedly replied.

Elder Boone answered, "You are welcome. Have a good night."

Sister Jason's face didn't show very much excitement. With her dress unzipped, she walked back and forth, going nowhere. A little distracted, she kept repeating, "*Why* is she coming? *Why* is she coming--*here?*"

I was surprised by her words, and they resounded in my ears. I decided to sit down on the couch. I wanted to see her daughter, yet, I stayed quiet. I was afraid that she would not understand my desire to see Flo.

According to the clock on the kitchen wall, it was almost midnight. I continued to sit in cautious silence, trying to put the pieces to the puzzle together.

My New York mother sat on the couch beside me, and leaning forward, she suddenly said, "We won't be able to sleep late tomorrow as we usually do on Saturday mornings. My daughter, Flo, is coming from Teaneck, New Jersey tomorrow."

I said, "Okay," glancing at her, wondering how long she was going to stay up.

After sitting for a while longer, she got up, said her usual, "Goodnight," and moseyed off to her room.

The hour was late, but I went forward in grim determination and took my usual nightly bath.

Afterward, I lie awake for a while, wondering about Sister Jason's daughter. Very soon afterward, I was fast asleep.

~~~~~~~~~~

On Saturday morning, I was awakened by the buzzer, and thought it might be Flo.

My northern mother answered the busser and invited the person up to our apartment. As I listened to the voice, I could tell that it was Sister Boone. I heard her say, "It was late last night when you came in. I was just making sure you got your message."

Sister Jason replied, "Yes, I did."

The Sisters stood in the hallway near the door, and I could not hear the rest of their conversation. I got up and made my bed.

I was on my way to the bathroom when Sister Jason stopped me to finally tell me what was weighing on her mind. She said, "Sister Boone came over this morning. I think she wanted to find out where we were last night, but that isn't any of her business. She used the excuse about the telephone call that she got—yesterday—afternoon. Now, she was too busy watching those ole soapbox operas to take the time to come and tell me."

Being only seventeen-years-old, I continued being just a sounding board. I said, "Really?"

Now, I really meant, "**Really? The Elder's wife was watching Soap operas?**" That was a no-no for a Saint in the Church of God.

"Yes—really," Sister Jason pronounced distinctly. She then

went on to say, "She waited until Elder Boone came in from work—to send him over to give me the news."

I stood, waiting for her to say all that she had to say. She walked to the stove to attend to the breakfast foods. With her back to me, she said, as if she were talking to herself, "That man would do anything that woman asked him to do, and she doesn't even keep that apartment clean for him."

What she was saying was quite interesting, and I sure was enjoying the gossip.

When she had finished at the stove, she seemed to have come out of her spell. She turned to me suddenly and said in her familiar way, "Finish what you're doing; then, we'll eat our breakfast."

I sat at the table, and as always, she place my plate in front of me. We had scrambled eggs with chopped veggies sprinkled on top, along with a slice of toast.

I thought of how different my breakfast would be back in the south. I missed my grits and eggs. Our eggs came straight from the hen house. Many times, they were still warm when we gathered them.

Sister Jason seemed to believe that breakfast was the most important meal of the day. She was one to stand firm on her views.

During breakfast, I could tell that Sister Jason was nervously awaiting the visit from her daughter. Given the calmness of the room, I could even feel my heart beating while we anticipated the arrival.

We had almost finished cleaning up the kitchen when Flo arrived. She announced herself through the speaker, and Sister Jason let her in. The two ladies brushed by each other with a slight hug.

I was introduced to her, and she didn't seem too impressed. She went for the kitchen and pulled back a chair from the table. I had to keep myself from staring.

Flo wore heavy makeup, and was a little overweight, both of which were no-nos for Sister Jason.

Flo asked, "How are you doing Mama?"

"As well as you would expect," Sister Jason snapped, as she continued to find more to clean in the kitchen.

"Mama, are you still having those dizzy spells?" asked the daughter.

Looking away, Sister Jason answered, "Why would you care?"

Flo rolled her eyes, patted a foot, hummed, and looked away, as if to say, "Here we go again."

My jaw dropped, and my face must have clearly shown all the questions I knew better than to ask. So far, what I was seeing was not impressive. I had the feeling that this Mom and daughter did not get along very well.

As Sister Jason walked by Flo she looked down, and peering at the top of her daughter's head she asked, "Are you still putting that stuff— *relaxer*—in your hair?"

"Yes, I *like* it. It takes the tangles out of my hair," Flo said.

The lady stopped and looked at her, remarking, "You're going to keep on until you won't have any hair."

Flo took a quick breath, and then she said, "Mama, my hair is not as curly as yours."

"You have pretty hair, but you are messing it up with that stuff. *Just mark my word*," Sister Jason replied, as she took her stance, one hand placed firmly on her hip.

By that time, Flo seemed to be getting a little huffy. She flipped her hair and answered back, "I like my hair *straight*."

With a gospel undertone, her mother said, "If God had wanted you to have straight hair, he would have given you straight hair."

I knew that Flo was strong in spirit about who and what she wanted to be or do, when she said, "Don't worry Mama. I do consider what God has done and will do. As I have told you so *many* times, I will not be trapped in a **small** world."

"Oh, sometimes, I wonder about you," her Mama answered, waving her hand as she spoke, as if to shoo off whatever her daughter was insinuating.

I was feeling Sister Jason's strong desire to have her daughter be a part of the Church of God and be saved, sanctified, and living a life above sin. She truly seemed appalled at her own creation. I assumed the two women had had these kinds of conversations before I arrived on the scene, based on their responses to one another. The lines seemed like something they had each spoken and heard many times before, to no avail. Still, I was hoping things between them would cool down in my presence. I hated arguments; they tore my insides apart. On the other hand, in general, in regard to arguments, I think that I was the one to take things too seriously.

One thing was unmistakably clear—each of these ladies had long ago made up her mind not to agree with the other. As the minutes passed, the two agreeing on anything looked less and less likely, but thanks to a shared "great thirst", they both wanted a glass of lemonade.

Sister Jason made great lemonade, and carried a sense of pride about it, as she poured three glasses full.

The three of us sat at the kitchen table and sipped the delicious, cool drink, as if all was right with the world. I think I was the only one of the group that had not fully adapted to all that had been said in the apartment that morning.

Thanks to the ever-present clock on the kitchen wall, the daughter glanced at the time and announced that she would soon have to leave. Before departing, she left the kitchen for the bathroom. Sister Jason was completely silent the whole time her daughter was gone.

Flo had done some primping while in the bathroom. She came out with a replenished shade of red on her lips, and her hair was neatly combed into place.

As I observed Sister Jason, I could tell that she did not care for Flo's style of living. As a parent, she probably had acted in the same way many of the other Church of God folks typically did when dealing with their children. She had most likely put lots of rules into effect and made it crystal clear that certain things were not permissible. Flo had probably been given many speeches on what was truth, justice, morality and virtue, and those things that were the direct opposites of truth, justice, morality and virtue, must be avoided at all costs.

When it was time for Flo to go, she gave her mother a quick peck on the cheek and was out the door. From what I could see, she didn't seem to be suffering unduly from the absence of her mother's companionship. I must say, she exhibited much strength and endurance.

After Flo had gone, Sister Jason quickly recovered, acting like she normally did, quickly, settling into her normal daily routine.

At the end of the afternoon, Sister Jason and I prepared for our trip to the baptism ceremony in Washington, DC. A bus would be leaving from the church early the next morning, but as usual, we were not going on the church bus. We were riding with the Boones.

~~~~~~~~~~

I was jolted out of a deep sleep. I jerked upright and looked around. Sister Jason was standing in my doorway. She said, "Good morning, we should be up and getting ready for our trip to DC."

In no time, I was up and ready. Our breakfast was French toast, bacon, and milk.

After cleaning the kitchen, we grabbed our bags and were out the door. A light breeze was in the air as we crossed the street to the Boone's apartment. Sister Jason made an announcement into the speaker, "We're out here on the stoop."

I heard, "Okay, we'll be out soon."

After a good while, Elder Boone, Sister Boone, and the two children—Susan and Mia—came out the door.

We all got into the car; and, we had gone several blocks when Sister Boone announced, "I don't have my glasses!"

Elder Boone replied, "We are running a little late. We want to get there before those buses start rolling in."

Sister Boone answered, "But, I won't be able to read anything without my glasses."

Her husband looked at her, and then took a right turn. He announced, "We'll just go back and get them then."

Sister Jason gave me an "I told you so" look.

On the trip to Washington, I observed everything around me. Elder Boone was a little easy going with Sister Boone. On the other hand, from my observations of him in church, I knew he had an inner strength and a strong faith in God. He was one whose complacent nature in dealing with his family belied the strength of character he showed in the pulpit.

The baptism in the Church of God in Washington, D.C. was a significant event that took place each year. It captured the attention of thousands.

By the time we reached the church on Georgia Avenue, a crowd had already gathered. Later, the many church buses paraded into Griffin Park. They hailed from New York, Philadelphia, Baltimore, Union Bridge and New Port News, Virginia. They were covered with inspirational words, photos of Elder Copeland, and of course, biblical verses.

While we was getting dressed for baptisms, we received assistance from some of the Sisters who were on duty. One particular lady scrambled across the room to assist me. She introduced herself as "Sister Greene", and said that she was from the state of New Jersey. In fact, she let me know that she had attended Elder Copeland's Church of God in New York for a short while and was acquainted with Sister Jason. She seemed aware of the fact that I was staying with the Sister. After her introduction, she seemed deep in thought, as she narrowed her eyebrows, and worked without saying another word.

I said very little, not really knowing what to say. Though, I wasn't sure, I strongly suspected that she wanted to know more about Sister Jason and me.

Later, all the baptismal candidates were dressed in white, from head to toe. We filed in to receive our Christian rites of significance and importance. We publicly received a personal faith in Jesus Christ in a water baptism. One by one, we were immersed. Every candidate had been born again and were now being baptized as a symbol of the fact that he or she was a child of God.

Later, when I was in the dressing room, Sister Greene came in to see me. Right away, she asked, "Did you travel here on the bus with the youth group?"

Of course, my answer was, "No."

She looked as if she were contemplating on how to say what she intended to say. Finally, she took a deep breath, and then asked, "How are the two ladies getting along?"

I suspected whom she was speaking of, but inquired, "Which two ladies?"

"Sister Jason and Sister Little," she boldly announced.

"I don't know," I answered.

"Did Sister Little ask you to join the youth group?" Sister Greene asked.

"No," I answered, but she waited, clearly wanting more of a response, so I added, "She has never said anything to me."

She turned her face away and said, as if she were talking to herself, "So . . .those two *still* can't get along."

I waited for her to say more, but she simply stared silently at the door behind me.

I turned around and saw Sister Jason coming our way. She didn't seem very pleased to see me conversing with Sister Greene. She quickly asked, "Why is it taking you so long to dress? We have to go, so that you can get ready for work tomorrow."

Sister Jason put her hand on me and gave me a slight push away from Sister Greene. That was the first time she had physically touched me when she was angry. She had not expertly managed her emotions, embarrassing me in front of the Sister that way.

Sister Greene merely shook her head, and walked away, headed in the opposite direction.

My eyes threatened to puddle, and I was visibly shaken. I

think the lady could read my displeased body language. Just maybe, she was afraid that I might play defense. She did not attempt to clutch my arm as she usually did, so that I could support her on the way to the car. Instead, she struggled in front of me, making her own way. I followed behind her, even when the old lady had to fight her way through a particularly troublesome spot that was mushy and grassy. When we reached the car, Susan and Mia pushed and played with the doorknob. Each wanted to be the one to open the door.

Sister Jason had stopped and was holding onto the car for support, while she tried to get her breath. She then tried to get the playful girls' attention, but to no avail. They only discontinued their game when the door came open, whereupon, each claimed to be the winner.

On our ride back to New York City, everyone was exceedingly quiet. Susan and Mia spent the time sleeping. I drifted off a few times, too.

We arrived in the brightly lit city just after midnight. Sister Jason was kinder to me than ever. I could see an apology in all that she did to assist me in getting ready for bed. She thought of me as a sleepyhead. After all, I did love to sleep, and would have to punch in at work later that same morning.

~~~~~~~~~~

At work, I noticed everyone seemed to be the happiest they'd been since I'd known them. They were all in the best of moods, and the fascinating conversations they were engaged in were all about getting ready for the upcoming Macy's Thanksgiving Day Parade. I admired the way the employees worked together to assist in preparing for the parade.

I knew that it was pointless to try to change Sister Jason's rules. She had said that I was to come stretch home each day, and she would have dinner ready.

I was beginning to feel more like her "little doll" rather than her "little girl".

Ellen had success in spearheading the many late evening parade work sessions. She encouraged all the ladies in our department to take part in the fun-filled evenings. Her expression was, "The cherry on the top of it all will be the exceptional foods."

Workers' union meetings were also held after work, and most of the employees put the meetings on their "must do" list. Dan, the union representative, did an exceptional job in keeping us abreast of the latest developments. I sensed that Mr. Laughton had informed Dan about Nellie Jason and her little girl, that, she was to come straight home after work each day. Laughton and Jason sure seemed close enough to share ideas.

Since we had to pay deductible dues, I made a powerful effort to understand the value of the workers' union. Just maybe, it was not so strange that I just didn't like the money being taken from my check. I wanted every penny of my money to go toward my college fund.

After work that Monday evening, Ellen and I got on the elevator together. I was afraid that she still might have been drumming up support for the parade, the workers' union, or maybe some other activity. I tried to ignore her, but she did recognize my presence in the corner, and said, "I understand that it was raining outside earlier."

I exclaimed, "It was?"

"There might be some lightning, too," she said, perhaps in an effort to keep the conversation going.

"I hope not," I replied. I was afraid that my talking with her might heighten her awareness that I had never socialized with the other workers, and that I hadn't joined in with any of their activities that weren't directly work related. I checked the number above the door of the elevator. Never had it taken an elevator so long to descend to the ground floor. When the door finally slid open, I darted out. Once out on the street, I took a deep breath. However, I really should have known that Ellen would not have badgered me. She was too smart for that.

I walked down 34th Street. The rain had let up, but the storm-brewing clouds continued to linger overhead. I was in a courageous frame of mind. I thought I might just ask Sister Jason if I could stay after work to assist with preparing for the parade. After all, she was a Thanksgiving Parade fan. Did I not hear her say - that – she never missed a Thanksgiving Parade?

Once I was on the train and began to mull over the idea, I thought it wouldn't be a good decision. The main reason I came to the city was to make my dream of going to college come true. Once again, I took a good look at my situation and my needs. It was very clear that making any adjustments might get me moving in the wrong direction.

By the time the train came to my stop, I had finished my therapeutic session with myself. I sprang off of the train and up the transit steps. I could see from that distance that the lady was standing on the steps waiting for me. I became fully aware that there was no way she would want me to come home at night all by myself. I realized that no matter what, I was still her—"little girl from the South."

Dinner was ready. The distinct aroma told me that a cinnamon apple pie was prepared. In no time, we were sitting in our usual places, opposite one another. Sister Jason blessed the food, and the moment the prayer was completed, she asked, "What were you and Sister Greene talking about yesterday?"

The lady had been concise in her question. I wasn't a bit surprised that she asked me about my conversation with Sister Greene. In fact, I had already given some thought to what my response to the anticipated question would be. I replied, "She wanted to know if I had joined the youth group."

"That's not her business," Sister Jason answered, snidely; then, in the same breath, she asked, "And what else did she want to know?"

The corner of my mouth curled as I said, "That's all." I was trying to convince her, but I could tell, she wasn't satisfied.

She rested her fork on her plate, and then said, "You two

talked for a good while."

I stammered as I answered, "It – it – wasn't that long. We just talked all about the youth group."

With a lopsided smile, she stated, "Sister Little was at the baptism. She should have asked *her* about the youth group—not you!"

"She could have. Ah - I don't know," I said, fervently hoping that was the end of that conversation.

Sister Jason took a mouthful of food. She chewed thoughtfully, swallowed, and then said, "That lady lives right over there in New Jersey, but only comes to church every once in a blue moon. It's no wonder she doesn't know what's going on. Then too, she felt the need to go all the way to Washington, DC, to work in the dressing room. I just don't understand some of these people."

The conversation was veering down another trail. I wanted to speak—to say something, but I didn't know *what* to say. I thought of Sister Jason's lonely situation and her need to talk, so I just shrugged and replied, "Uh-huh."

Everything was quiet. The ticking of the clock seemed louder than ever. Sister Jason looked up from her plate the very moment I looked up from my own. We both cracked a smile.

As my Dad would say, "Sometimes we have to tie loose ends together before we can move on."

13 CHAPTER THIRTEEN

MAE

As we express our gratitude,

we must never forget that the highest

appreciation is not to utter words,

but to live by them.

~ John F. Kennedy

The following weekend, on a windy Fall Saturday afternoon, Sister Jason and I made our usual trip to the food shop around the corner. The lady had discovered that I was not a finicky eater; therefore, she felt free to buy whatever foods she desired.

As always, the butcher did not hesitate to give "Mrs. Jason" the best cuts of meat, at a reduced price. Not only did she get the best of service from the butcher, but I was there at her beck and call, reaching for the high-up items, bending for the items down low and pulling the food cart around the store behind us.

Sister Jason loved to cook, and we feasted sumptuously, but not excessively. She was all about food balancing.

Once again, we left the shop with our cart bulging. I pulled it through the streets. As I walked, I could see people between two tall buildings. They were talking and giggling. I glimpsed a man's profile, and I stopped to see what was going on. Then, I saw someone in front of him. Before I could see more, Sister

Jason insisted, "Don't stop! Keep moving! Just ignore them."

I took a deep breath, and even looked back while I stumbled toward the apartment. My face must have been all questions, as the lady shushed me along.

My mind was still racing as I lugged the cart up the steps. Standing at the top, I could see Sister Jason getting her breath on the bottom step. A few minutes later, she came to the top and opened the mail box. She handed me a letter.

The letter was addressed to: Miss Mae Etta Bloomfield. I speechlessly blinked at the envelope while I read my sister's name which was clearly written above the return address. My sister, who was living in Washington, D.C., had written to me. I uttered loudly, "A letter from my sister! Mama must have given her my address!"

I stepped to the side, slowly turning the envelope over with my hands and viewing it from different angles. Sister Jason was looking over my shoulder. She kept her voice low when she said, "We could go inside and read it." I grabbed the cart with one hand, while holding the envelope securely in the other. I moved toward the elevator.

When the elevator reached the second floor, I hopped off and made my way to number two-forty-seven. I inhaled deeply and slowly exhaled while waiting for the lady to open the door. It seemed like she was taking her own good time.

When we were finally inside, Sister Jason released me from my job as her assistant. She said, "You go on and read your letter. I will put the groceries away."

Without hesitation, I strode to my room, closed the door, and carefully opened the letter.

The letter read:

Dear Mae Etta,

How are you doing? I am well and doing fine. I am sorry that I was not able to come to your baptism. I had to work. I am still a bus girl at the Hot Shoppe in Bethesda, Maryland. My boss is talking to me about the possibility of becoming a waitress. He wants to move some of the black girls up to the position of waitress. We have already discussed some of the forces that we would be up against and know they would be vocal in their opposition; but, I am ready and willing to move forward. I hope it happens soon because I need to make more money than I am currently making.

Aunt Maggie said that she saw you get baptized but was not able to get with you before you left for New York.

Jasper Jackson is still writing to me. We sort of got engaged before he left. He gave me his class ring as an engagement ring.

I wish I could see you. I miss you so very much.

Your sister,

Ida Lee

My happiness escalated as I read the letter. When I had finished, I went to the kitchen where Sister Jason seemed to be waiting for me. I was eager to share my joyful news.

I said, "My sister misses me and wants to see me!"

In a very thoughtful manner, Sister Jason replied, "Maybe she should come to New York to see you."

I felt so delighted. I replied with a question, "Really?"

"Yes. Why not?" She asked in turn.

I was so pleased that my New York mother had proposed the idea. I answered, "I will write her right now and invite her to come." I then raced to my bedroom to get paper and pencil. I came out and sat at the kitchen table and began writing.

Dear Ida Lee,

I received your letter. I was so happy to learn that you are well and doing fine. I am also doing well and enjoying my new job.

We left Washington, D.C. as soon as the baptism was over because some of us had to get back for work the next day. I am sorry that you could not attend. I was looking forward to seeing you and Aunt Maggie. There were so many people, and I did not want to get lost in the crowd.

Sister Jason suggested that you should come to New York to see us. Please let me know as soon as possible if you can come.

I miss you so much, and I will be waiting to hear from you very soon.

Your sister,

Mae Etta

As I addressed my envelope and placed the three-cent stamp on it, I had a feeling that everything was developing in a wonderful direction.

~~~~~~~~~~~~~

The weekend came when Sister Jason and I went to Yankee Stadium to see Billy Graham. I had a feeling that many of the Saints in Church would not have approved of such an excursion. They had a philosophical belief that the teaching of their church was the right and only path to heaven. The people in the church did not have a desire to follow others in any way shape, form or fashion.

All the members seemed to have believed in the faith of their pastors, who fed and strengthened them in their faith, with the word of God.

From my understanding, and from what I could see, the church was built on strong friendships and great personal relationships. The Church of God fed the hungry, healed the sick and attended the wounded. I was told that they even had apartments in Virginia to shelter the homeless.

On our trip to the stadium, we took a bus. I was deep in thought as we rode along. Not a word was said between the two of us.

After exiting the bus, Sister Jason clung to my arm, as we scuffled down a trail of steps. When we reached the bottom, we stumbled headlong, while all the bright lights in the stadium shone down on us.

At that point in our excursion, I gave our trip serious thought: *Sister Jason was bent on making this trip. She was surely one who believed in herself. When a big decision loomed, she followed her heart. I admired her self-reliance. I was sure that she used those self-skills when she invited me — someone, she had never met - into her home in New York City.*

After we had wrestled our way to the seating area, we

struggled to find two empty seats together. When we did discover the two seat, I ran ahead and grabbed them. Sister Jason joined me. We, then, relaxed, took in a breath of air and looked around the stadium.

We were seated for a while when the crowd slightly settled in the big opened area. Then we heard the introduction of Evangelist Billy Graham. The crowd received him with thunderous applause.

While listening to the minister, Sister Jason nodded her head, smiled and whispered a soft, "amen." Her heart and mind were seemingly touched by his words.

As for me, I was mesmerized by the crowd and the diverse mixture of races represented in the throng of people. For a while, my mind was stuck in observation zone. The question on my mind was: **How could one person get so many followers?** Then, I shifted my mind to listen, and had a conscious awareness of what was being said. I heard him say, "Our nation was founded by men who believed in prayer. In his address to the 1787 Constitutional Convention, founding father Benjamin Franklin asserted, "God governs in the affairs of men."

Almost everyone had their eyes closed when Billy Graham said the closing prayer. When the prayer ended, the crowd lifted their hands and a chorus of "Amen" rang out loud and clear.

We returned home on the bus. Sister Jason's spirit had been lifted to a new height. She recited the history of Yankee Stadium for me, and said that she had attended the inaugural game, when the Yankees vs Boston Red Socks on April 18, 1923.

She seemed to get a second thought and asked if I would like to attend a baseball game at Yankee Stadium.

As I recalled the boys playing baseball at school, I graciously replied, "I would love to go to a baseball game."

Smiling as if she were in love, she said, "Roy Campanella is my favorite baseball player. He lives in Glen Cove, New York, but he owns a store in Harlem.

I inquired, "What team does he play for?"

"The Brooklyn Dodgers, of course," she answered. Then, she asked, "Do you know anything about baseball?"

With a feeling of gratitude, I announced, "My daddy taught me a lot about baseball. Sometimes he would play with us in the backyard." I was so excited to tell her more about my daddy. My New York mother had discovered that my parents were very special to me. She was also aware that I was hoping that one day I would be able to give them some of things they deserved in life.

~~~~~~~~~~

It was almost November, and the anticipation was building for the Macy's Thanksgiving Day Parade as a ritual to herald in the holiday season. The employees embraced the idea of having any micro-part to play in the great tradition. As for me, my mind was on something else. Each day, I looked forward to the prospect of receiving a letter from my sister. I desired my sister's visit; and yet, I was on pins and needles about my New York mother's behavior. She had her way of bringing out the worst in some people. More precisely, one needed to have lived in the home for a while to truly understand her. She had a generous heart, but she was way too straight-forward.

It happened on a Thursday evening. Ida Lee wrote to me, giving her answer to my question. Yes, she was coming to New York to visit; she would be coming on November 2nd, which would be about two weeks from the present date. I felt that things had changed as if through magic. If only the 'magic' would last for a while.

Sister Jason suggested that we call her Ida. She said that she preferred to drop middle names.

The matter was all "never-mind" for me. I noticed she had

dropped my middle name in conversation right after we first met. I got the "up north" picture of it all.

The lady did share my delight when I announced that Ida was coming. To my dismay, she even assisted in the planning of our activities. She asked, "Would she be interested in seeing a Broadway play?"

I shrugged and replied, "We have only seen plays at school, but I think I would like that."

"The question is, do you think *she* would like it?" she asked.

"She would like what I like," I answered, without a doubt in my mind.

Sister Jason looked at me with a wry face and folded arms, as she asked, "Are you sure?"

I was so excited that I almost reverted to saying, "Sho' nuf," but I gave my reply a second thought and simply said, "I'm sure."

"I was just throwing out an idea," my New York mother explained.

I replied, "I think it's a good idea."

"Oh okay, we'll see," she said.

After dinner, we continued to plan for the weekend of Ida's visit, as Sister Jason proposed many other ideas. I took the many ideas to bed and mulled them over before falling off to sleep.

The very next day, I received another letter from Ida Lee. She wanted to spend the weekend of the visit going to Long Island to see our uncle. She said that Mama wanted us to visit Uncle Paul.

Now, Uncle Paul was one person in my Daddy's family that he accepted. For some unknown reason, he received Paul as a brother whenever he visited from New York.

After reading the letter, I made an assumption that Sister Jason would not go along with such plan. Mentally, I even opposed the plan. In no way did I want to antagonize my New York mother; the last thing I wanted was a protracted argument. I even found it difficult to verbally explain my sister's suggestion to the lady.

That afternoon, we were cleaning the kitchen together, and I took a unique approach to tell Sister Jason about what my sister had suggested. I said, "I have an uncle who lives on Staten Island.

"He's—

Before I could finish, she looked up from wiping crumbs off the table and asked, "How long has he lived there?"

I answered, "As long as I can remember."

She said, "You should have mentioned it. Maybe we could have visited him."

"Does he have a wife and children?" she asked.

"No children, but I don't know about a wife," I said, and after a few seconds, I continued, "Ida wants to go to Staten Island to visit Uncle Paul."

To my surprise, Sister Jason replied, "Then you should go to see him."

My mouth opened, but no words came out. As my mother would have said, "You could have knocked me over with a feather." The lady had voiced her approval and support.

While I was still in profound disbelief, she asked me for the address.

I raced to my bedroom, retrieved the letter, and read the address to her.

When I finished reciting it, Sister Jason explained the directions to Staten Island to me, but I am sure she was aware that giving me that information was like the proverbial, "Pouring water on a duck's back."

The following night, I had sweet dreams, and I arose early the next morning with happiness lurking in my heart.

When I returned from work, my New York mother had gone to the transit station to get more information on the directions we would need to follow to get to Staten Island by the ferry.

As I received the information, my thoughts went to something my mother use to say when her sisters and brothers agreed on something, "What a blessing to be bound together for a common cause."

~~~~~~~~~~~~~

The day of my sister's arrival in New York came. I woke up earlier than I had most mornings. I got out of bed feeling very energetic, and the feeling continued throughout the day.

After the work day, I took the train to the bus station to meet my sister. Sister Jason felt comfortable with my leaving work and connecting with her. Anyway, I had become an experienced traveler on the transit system around the Manhattan borough.

When I arrived at the bus station, my sister was waiting outside, with her suitcase by her side. I ran to her, and we grabbed hands, as we grinned and starred at each other. I was so excited as I said, "I can't believe you're here."

Ida exclaimed, "Oh, I can't believe I'm here—in—New York City! How are you doing? How is the lady treating you? Aunt Maggie has been worried about you."

I was surprisingly titillated by all the questions that only a dear sister might ask. I stated, "I'm fine. Really! Sister Jason is good to me—but, uh—uh—why is Aunt Maggie worried about me?"

Ida gave a pause, then said, "You know Aunt Maggie. She feels that nobody can do anything as well as she can. You know that she wanted you to join us in Washington, DC after you finished high school, don't you?"

"I know that," I said. "I made the decision to come here, and so far, I think I made the right decision. Things are different sometimes, but there is so much I like about being here."

"She wanted you to find her and speak to her, when you were in DC at the baptizing," Ida muttered, as if someone else was listening.

"I know—I know," I managed to say.

I was reminded of the fact that Sister Jason had put her hand on me in front of a Sister, and I was hoping that she did not tell Aunt Maggie about the incident. Trying to push the thought away, I grabbed Ida's hand and said, "Let's find the bus stop."

We found the bus stop, and on the ride home, we caught up on some of the family news. Ida told me that Buddy had left Uncle Ted's farm, and had come to Washington, DC. She let me know that she didn't care for the friends whom he had chosen, and she was worried about him.

My heart was heavy. I had heard about the things that were happening to some of the young boys in New York City. I had been told about the Gangs in the city. I felt a chill come over me. I thought about how much time buddy and I had spent together. He was my outdoors playmate – once upon a time, and I was hoping that he would straighten-up and do better.

~~~~~~~~~~~~~~~

We arrived at the apartment before dark. Sister Jason was very cordial and greeted Ida with warmth and grace. After the introductions were made, we carried Ida's luggage to my bedroom. Ida glanced around the apartment as we prepared for dinner. The dinner was grilled chicken, creamed potatoes, steamed green beans, and spiced apple turnovers.

As dinner began, I was very quiet and filled with fright that Sister Jason might smart mouth my sister. I even bit my lower lip and was silent.

Sister Jason might have noticed that I was a little nervous. We ate and sat at the kitchen table, drinking lemonade, and talking long after dinner was over. Contrary to what I had thought might happen, Sister Jason responded pleasantly throughout our conversation.

I was surprisingly titillated by the possibility that Ida could only make a pleasant report to Mama about my stay in New York. At that point, she could only say pleasing things about

Sister Jason. Surely, she could tell her that I was placed in a job that was well suited for me, and one that I highly enjoyed.

Dinner long over and the hour being late, we all went off to bed. Ida and I talked well into the night.

We arose early on Saturday morning to prepare for our trip to Staten Island. Uncle Paul was expecting us. Ida had gotten in touch with him by telephone.

As we dressed for our trip, we coordinated our outfits as much as possible. Mama had taught us that we were beautiful young ladies and should wear our styles effortlessly. We should not be concerned about trends. She would say, "Don' worry 'bout what's in Sears Roebuck Catalogue for this season, or what's on Belk's hangers."

However, there were certain times, I didn't feel up-to-date or in style, but I kept it all under my hat.

Mama was so thankful that some unknown nice lady had directed her to the consignment store around the corner just before reaching Five Points. The store was off the beaten path, so much so that anyone not familiar with the area would never guess the store was there. Mama told us, "Be happy we found that second-hand store. Find something that looks good on you."

Mama wanted us to believe that self-confidence and a firm knowledge of who we are inside are the best, true foundations of great styles. When dressing, we should remember those principles and not lose that connection to our authentic selves. She reiterated, "You should feel good, look good, and act good in your clothes." She meant that clothes should be comfortable, wearable, durable, and of the highest quality, but you must have good behavior as well.

When I compared my clothing with what was in Macy's department store, I was pleasantly pleased with what I had in my wardrobe. I also found that I only needed a few warmer pieces. Sister Jason was very pleased that I had a plan for coordinating my resources and expenditures.

~~~~~~~~~~~~~~

Dressed up and looking good, Ida and I were out of the apartment and on our way to Staten Island. We even stopped at the photography studio to have pictures made. During our transit, we embraced the opportunity to polish our relationship. We discussed the fact that it was our responsibility to keep our relationship harmonious and intact. We both promised to write to each other often.

Uncle Paul met us at the ferry. We exchanged hugs as his face radiated with happiness. He welcomed us to the Staten Island borough. As we leisurely rode along on the way to his house, he said, "You might already know that there are five boroughs in New York; they are Manhattan, Brooklyn, Queens, the Bronx, and Staten Island. We call our borough "the forgotten borough." That is because sometimes we seem to be excluded in the city's planning."

I was taking in the view of the red and orange leaves when I heard Uncle Paul say, "The Fall season is the perfect time to visit Staten Island, so you two hit the nail on the head."

As we ventured toward our destination, our uncle brought a white stone building to our attention. He announced, "This is our historical Conference House."

Driving further, he said, "We are the least populated of the five boroughs. Staten Island is a suburban borough."

As I looked out the window, I could see the many suburban homes, but also saw country, in comparison to the other suburbs.

Shortly after disembarking from the ferry, we reached our uncle's white side-boarded house. Before we started up the driveway of his house, Uncle Paul pointed out more interesting autumn splendor. Our surroundings were breathtaking.

We crawled out of the car while he rushed up the steps to open the door. We strolled up the sidewalk onto a porch that had a few missing boards. When the weather-beaten door was flung open, we stepped inside. I could feel a sense of instant hush, but the feeling did not diminish the delicious aroma coming from the kitchen. As I glanced around the place, I could see that the house was spotlessly clean. He obviously was perfectly content, but the loneliness of the scene deeply affected me.

Uncle Paul announced, "I have prepared an early dinner for you. Ida Lee, you did tell me that you all could not spend the night. Did you not?"

We spoke almost simultaneously, "No, we can't spend the night."

"I hope you will like what I have cooked for you," our uncle said with a friendly smile.

Ida Lee replied, "Oh, we'll love whatever you have."

I said, "It sure smells good."

My stomach fluttered as I waited for someone to appear from the next room. When Uncle Paul turned his back to get food from the stove, I looked at Ida Lee and raised my eyebrows, expressing my uncertainty.

My sister gave me a nod.

In a little while, our uncle put a pork roast with gravy and a bowl of black-eyed peas on the table. He told us to dive in.

As we scooped up our food, I thought I heard a movement in the house. Ida Lee gave me an eye that told me that she heard it, too.

I bit my lower lip, as I was feeling there was something spooky about this house. When we first arrived, I could sense there was something in this house akin to that other house we had once lived in back in North Carolina. In our past experiences in that old house, we had seen odd happenings and had heard mysterious sounds. We swore that the house was haunted. From that time on, we have all believed in ghosts.

When we had finished our meal, we sat on the sofa in the front room. As Uncle Paul grunted and slowly sat down, he said, "I'm glad that you two have come to see me. I just got out of the hospital not too long ago."

I asked, "Hospital?"

Ida asked, "Are you okay?"

He shook his head and said, "I wish I could rewind the whole thing, but certain things are not possible."

"What happened?" Ida inquired before he could answer her first question.

"Oh, I wasn't giving the highway as much attention as I should have. I was tired and should have gotten more rest before going on my trip," Uncle Paul told us.

Of course, I was happy to find him still alive. I wanted to know more about my Daddy's family.

I asked, "Do you know very much about your family?"

"Yes, I do. What-a ya want to know?" he stuttered.

"Tell us about Daddy's family," Ida added.

Uncle Paul looked distracted. Then, he said, "Now, that's a different story."

I didn't know what to say, and I was sure that Ida Lee didn't either. There was so much that we didn't know about our Daddy's family. We were chock full of nips of stories, some good, but most not so good. The tidbits of this and that changed from mouth to mouth. I really wanted to ask questions, but I didn't know how to put them into words.

When Uncle Paul sat in deep thought and dropped his jaws, he looked so much older.

My insides kind of collapsed. I think Ida Lee felt his pain also. She stood and said, "I think it is time for us to go back to Manhattan. Thank you for the dinner."

I said, "The dinner was delicious. Thanks so much."

All the while, we were shaking hands.

Just as we were leaving, Uncle Paul's heart radiated a generous spirit. He handed us each a twenty-dollar bill.

I had not expected such a generous gift. We both bent forward with our thanks.

Our uncle delighted us by telling hilarious family stories, as he drove us to the ferry boat. All the stories were pleasantly boxed and wrapped with a bow. I almost corrected him when he walked the tight line on a story about Sadie. We knew our aunt well, and we had seen her live a wild, reckless life, but I did agree that she had guts and determination.

We were let off at the ferry. We sailed happily toward the Manhattan borough.

~~~~~~~~~~~~~

Back at the apartment, we took a pass on dinner, and accepted a glass of lemonade. With no hesitation, we were off to bed. We were aware of the fact that we had a busy day ahead of us. Ida would be getting a bus back to D.C., and Sister Jason and I were going to church.

Early the next morning, I heard the alarm clock and couldn't believe the morning had come so soon. I rolled over and slowly pulled myself out of bed. Ida stretched, yawned, and then joined me. We made the bed together for old time's sake. In no time, we were ready.

Sister Jason had breakfast ready. I loved setting the table. Sister Jason had all the dishes and flatware needed to complete table setting the way I had learned it in my homemaking class at my high school.

Afterward, the three of us sat down to a very nutritious breakfast.

Later, I traveled with Ida back to the bus station. I waved at Ida as the Greyhound bus drove away from the station.

Ida waved back, giving me her most engaging smile and revealing her white teeth.

As I walked away toward the transit, I knew I would miss Ida and her good-humored nature.

I reached the church early, before Sister Jason arrived. The young man, Nelson, who had given me angled looks and smiles, was standing outside. As I approached, he gave me a penetrating look, and I wanted to melt into the sidewalk.

He said, "Good morning," and then hesitantly asked, "Where is Sister Jason?"

I answered, "She is coming. I went to the bus station to see my sister off."

He seemed so surprised to learn that I had a sister in town for the weekend.

We talked for a few minutes, really saying nothing. I enjoyed listening to him. His words were so clear. However, he had not lived up to my expectations, with such small talk.

He said that he had to be off to Sunday school, and he invited me to come along. I followed him to the room, which I had never entered before. The youth group was gathered, and I had my first real talk with Sister Little. Of course, she had spoken to me in passing.

Sister Little said, "I would love for you to be a part of the youth group, but I understand if you don't."

I said, "I'll let you know if I decide."

She asked, "Are you permitted to decide?"

I was thinking about what to say when Sister Jason entered the room.

She said, "Good Morning,"– really not looking at anyone. She then looked at me and asked, "Did Ida get off okay?"

I said, "Yes. I miss her already."

She said, "So do I. She was such a pleasant person."

We both moved out of the side room and into the sanctuary. One of the young ladies in the church caught up with us and said, "Sister Jason and Mae, I would like to ask you something."

Sister Jason, in her cantankerous voice, asked, "Yes, what?"

Gwen, who was used to Sister Jason's ways, said in her soft voice, "I would like to know if Mae would consider being a bride's maid in my wedding."

I opened my mouth to speak, but then took a look at my New York mother.

Sister Jason said, "Now, you know you can if you want to."

I answered, "Yes, I would love to."

Gwen said, "I'll get back to you to give you the details, but I will tell you now that it's going to be a snowball wedding in January of next year."

I was so excited to be a part of something—just anything! I couldn't keep my mind on the service. The thought of Gwen's asking me to be a bride's maid was so flattering. I was so exhilarated I had to push my pause button, breathe, and relax to settle down.

14 CHAPTER FOURTEEN

MAE

If you are going to achieve

excellence in big things,

you develop the habit in little matters.

Excellence is not an exception,

it is a prevailing attitude.

~ Colin Powell

All the way home, on the bus and down the street to our apartment, Sister Jason seemed to be in deep thought. When she reached the steps, she dropped her head, as she hung onto the side of the stoop. While making her way up the steps, she finally spoke. She uttered, "I just don't understand that young girl, wanting to marry that country boy."

I quietly followed her through the door and to the elevator. I pushed the button, and then glanced at Sister Jason's narrowed eyes. It suddenly dawned on me how seriously she was taking the matter of the wedding. The older women seemed to be carrying an unnecessary burden; however, there was nothing I could say or do about the matter.

The elevator door opened, and we slowly walked in. She glanced at me, which indicated that I should push the button.

On the short, quiet ride up to the second floor, I could hear the lady breathing, and the squeaking of the elevator was also clearly heard.

Neither of us had any desire to talk on the walk from the elevator to the door. We opened the door, went in, and went straight to our bedrooms.

Once in my room, I really didn't know what to do after I had removed my Sunday clothes, and slipped into something comfortable. So, I sat on the side of my bed, and gave much thought as to how I should receive the lady's words of disenchantment about the upcoming wedding. I swallowed hard and looked around the room, wondering how long I could sit there before Sister Jason would knock, or simply open the door.

After a few minutes–like an instant–I got up and went into our usual sitting room.

Sister Jason was resting comfortably on the couch. She looked up at me, gave me a quick glance, and then, she looked back at her magazine.

I sat down on the other end of the couch in my usual spot. When I glanced up at the lady, it seemed to give her permission to speak. She reiterated, "Poor Gwen, she sure wants to get married badly. She doesn't know very much about that boy she is planning to marry. He hasn't been in the church long enough. Many of those boys come to the church just to get our girls, and later on, they take them out."

I sat mum, for I was very thrilled that Gwen was having a wedding. I was ready and waiting to be one of the participants. My mind was wired up, and I wanted to scream, "Let the show go on! Let the party begin!"

The lady continued, "Gwen is such a sweet girl. I don't know how she puts up with that group she's always with. She gives such beautiful testimonies." Then, all in one breathe, she changed the topic, and asked, "Why don't you ever testify?"

I had known that question would be coming my way; and yet, I was not prepared to answer it. I struggled to reply. I opened my mouth, but nothing came out.

Sister Jason asked, "Is it because you don't think you're ready?"

I stammered, "No—no, I just hadn't thought about it." But, the truth was, I had thought about it. I simply couldn't think of another answer to give to her, at least not in that moment.

"When are you going to think about it? You're Saved, aren't you?"

I answered, "Yah-ah—yes."

"Then you should testify," the lady said in her demanding way.

Now, the last thing I wanted to do was to stand up in that church and talk. In fact, the thought of standing and talking in church had become an incredible nightmare for me. I really felt that I was being thrust into an uncomfortable situation. I just wished she would leave well enough alone.

~~~~~~~~~~~~~

The next week flew by. Nothing special really happened. All week, I put most of my thoughts into Sister Jason's testimony request. I thought about taking a wait-and-see attitude. My Dad always said, "It is best not to leap into something just because someone is using persistent persuasion." On the other hand, to steady myself, I tried relegating some words to memory, so I would be prepared, just in case I decided to give testimony that Sunday. Later, I had the sinking feeling that my few memorized remarks were not sticking to my brain.

On Sunday morning, while I was dressing for church, I sorted through all the circumstances. I thought it best that I stop contemplating "the ifs, ands, or buts" of whether I would go through with it, and instead, truly commit myself to choosing some sound words to deliver.

On that particular Sunday in November, we rode to church with Elder and Sister Boone. I felt vulnerable. I thought that maybe Elder Boone or Sister Boone had discussed my reluctance to testify with Sister Jason. There was one thing I knew for certain: my New York mother would always cover for me. After all, I was surely a reflection of her.

As always, when we reached the church, Elder Boone rushed around the car to assist Sister Boone out of the car. Of course, I assisted Sister Jason.

I was greatly impressed by the Elder's kindness and courtesy to all of the ladies in the church. He seemed a perfect gentleman. He behaved exactly as the gentlemen were taught to in our Social Graces Club at my high school.

Church began with the playing of music and singing of songs as usual, and then, the testimonies began. All kinds of fears surfaced in my mind, but I managed to stand. I was graced by the words that I had memorized.

When I sat, Sister Jason rose to give her testimony. As always, she told the Saints how blessed she was to have a wonderful, Saved girl staying with her. She closed with her usual: "I want you all to pray for Mae and me, that we will be all that God would have us to be."

After church, I received many more handshakes and blessings than usual.

On the way home, the elder and his wife complimented me on the beauty of my testimony.

I expressed my gratitude, but still felt that I should not have been obligated to mimic what others were doing.

When we reached the apartment, I went to my bedroom and carefully placed my Bible beside my Webster's Dictionary. I wasn't so naïve to think that my one-time testimony would solve the problem; I knew it was a temporary solution.

All of a sudden, I became buoyant at the idea of making application to the Winston-Salem Teachers College for the following fall semester. I scooped up my dictionary and turned to the back of the book. There, I found the Colleges and Universities' section, and I copied down all of the necessary information about the said college. After writing my request for an application, I thanked them in advance, and then, I sealed and stamped the envelope.

As I placed my dictionary back onto the dresser, I looked in the mirror and the reflection of my face revealed how pleased I was by the step I had just taken. I felt that maybe, I had just moved one step closer to attaining my educational goal.

~~~~~~~~~~~~~~

`Over the next couple of weeks, the month of November brought in the cold weather. On Thanksgiving Day, Sister Jason and I wrapped up in our wintery outfits and made our way to 34th Street. We found the perfect spot in front of Macy's Department Store. As we stood under the image of the turkey, we waited for the parade to start. Sister Jason and I joined a couple of my co-workers, with whom we discussed the history of the Macy's Thanksgiving Day Parade.

We all agreed that the tradition had started back in 1924. From that year forward, more balloons were subsequently added to the parade each year. The parade was suspended from 1942 through 1944 as a result of World War II—owing to the need for rubber helium to support the war effort. The annual festivities were broadcast on local radio stations in New York City from 1932 through 1941, resuming in 1945, and running through 1951. The three-hour Macy's event began being televised in 1952, premiering on NBC.

As the colorful parade appeared in the far distance, cheering arose from the delighted crowd. When the parade reached the department store, Mickey Mouse, Felix the Cat, and Bobo the Clown waved high in the wind, while the Fire Breathing Dragon, a cuddly looking black and white Teddy Bear, Lucky Pup, and Mighty Mouse flapped along. With its long body and short legs, the Dachshund followed. There was the Spaceman, who had made his first appearance in 1935. Marching merrily on their way were the Toy Soldiers, along with Uncle Sam. Of course, Pinocchio came alive in 1940. He was no longer a wooden puppet; he was a real balloon boy, who was well-behaved in the air. Soaring overhead was the Flying Fish, flipping like, what else? A fish out of water. The Acrobat balloon was of course, tossing and turning in the air.

When the amusement and delightedness were at their height, the presenter, Dave Garraway, who had held the position since 1952, introduced the newest parade balloon to the excited assembled crowd. A wave of enthusiastic cheers went up, when Popeye, made his first parade appearance, right there in 1957.

Santa Claus, of course, had been with the parade since its inception, and was in high spirits, welcoming us all, and wishing everyone a, "Merry Christmas."

The course of the day was slipping away, and Sister Jason's energy was well spent. As we left for 167th Street, I realized that being employed at Macy's Department Store had increased my range of perception enormously. Beforehand, I probably would not have noticed so many details of the beautiful balloons and decorations the parade had to offer. Also, I was no longer overwhelmed by the crowds and noises of the city.

I found that Thanksgiving was a very happy time. We set our prettiest table ever, using Sister Jason's old homemade fall centerpiece. We had observed the wonderful parade, returned home, and sat before a tender roast turkey, cornbread dressing, and mashed potatoes. I had even learned to eat Sister Jason's favorite spinach dish. Of course, she never knew how much I had always disliked the taste of spinach. By Thanksgiving Day, I had become accustomed to its taste, and was leaving the thoughts of the leafy mustard, turnip, and collard greens I had eaten regularly at home in North Carolina behind me.

~~~~~~~~~~~~~~

As December quickly approached, Gwen began to glow increasingly as the big day approached. If the fantastic glow she had was 'love', then her voyage must have been sensational. She had met with her wedding attendants, and her snowball wedding was well underway. Thank God, we had practice after prayer meeting on Wednesday nights. There was no way Sister Jason would have let me go to Harlem at night alone.

Gwen even shared her interesting life stories with us. She said that she had been content with her job, enjoyed what she did, had a busy church life, and enjoyed her big family, members of which she saw almost every day. She was the owner of her own small, and very charming apartment; yet, she wanted more. She went on to say, "Even though Arthur and I have dated for a short while, we were both looking for companions. When he asked me to marry him, I was silent for a while. I had to think about it, but I did say yes, as you all know, because, here we are—planning a wedding."

A laugh came roaring up from the group. I guess we were all just happy for Gwen, and sincerely wished her the very best.

When we met for practice, I would even suppress some of the happiness that flowed within me. Never would I have wanted Sister Jason to know how pleasurable I found it to be with the
Purity Club members. I did get an understanding that Elder Copeland's wife, Sister Copeland, organized the Purity Club years ago. Its purpose was to guide and instruct the youth. I was impressed when I heard the group repeat their motto: "Be a Peach Out of Reach. Remain Obedient. Have Love, Reverence, and Respect: first to God; second to Leadership; and then, to One Another."

Over the years, New York Purity Club groups had participated in numerus activities. Sometimes, they would travel to different church assemblies and perform various functions. Other times, each club would present programs at their home church. Sister Little was the present leader of the New York Church of God Purity Group, and unfortunately, she and Sister Jason did not see eye to eye; so, I was not allowed to join them. As for me, I had long been well aware that there was something going on between the two sisters. Sister Jason was not one to hide her disapproval. Anyway, whenever I got a chance, I kind a tried to fit in with the group as best I could without directly attracting the attention of Sister Jason, as I knew it would upset her. I had even gotten to know some of the young ladies and gentlemen, especially Gwen, who was the eldest of the group, and was pushing thirty years of age. She was a witty young lady, and I derived pleasure from her humor.

In one particular conversation with the young ladies, I learned that most of them had started their hope chests at an early age. I glanced at each person as she shared what had recently been added to her chest. I was fascinated with the word Sadie used: She called it her *trousseau*. It seemed there were all kinds of household goods stored away in the trousseau, in preparation, as each one anticipated the eventuality of entering into marriage and stepping into their new roles as wives.

After listening to that conversation, I decided that I wanted to begin a trousseau. Then, I gave the idea considerable thought, and realized that the idea was absurd. Sister Jason would surely spit fire, if I even mentioned such a venture. Sister Jason had mentioned to me—and *more than once*—that many of the girls in the church seemed happy to acquire a job after high school. She expressed her concern that they didn't seem to have any desire to pursue studies at colleges or universities for higher learning, despite the fact that there were so many in the city. Sister Jason had repeatedly said she wanted more than just a high school education for me (after all, that is why I had been invited to stay with her in NYC, to make money to make further education possible), and she wanted to make sure I let nothing interfere with my educational goals. And, of course, I desired more for myself, so we were of the same mind on this issue.

Yes, I enjoyed my job at Macy's doing keypunching; but, my greatest desire was still to go to a college or university—some institute of higher learning. Campus life seemed so fascinating; and, *oh*, how I dreamed of being a sorority girl! I did so appreciate all of Sister Jason's assistance; so, upon practical reflection, I decided to drop the idea of a trousseau until after my educational goals had been met, or at the very least, until I was well on my way to becoming the teacher I had resolved to become.

~~~~~~~~~~~~~~

I was so wrapped-up in the coming wedding, I had forgotten about my request for an application from Winston-Salem Teachers College. Out of the blue, all of my information arrived in the mail. The letter had gone unnoticed until after we had gotten home from prayer meeting.

When Sister Jason became aware of the fact that I had requested an application from the school in North Carolina, she suggested that I should give some consideration to a college in New York before returning the application.

My mind was so set on going to school in North Carolina, I couldn't help but disagree and said, "I want to complete the application and send it back as soon as I can."

There was a long silence before the lady asked, "Why do you want to go back down South?"

"That was my plan when I first came," I replied.

Sitting there, in front of me, Sister Jason looked at me pleadingly, a sad expression in her eyes. She was watching me very closely as if to say, "Please don't make plans to leave me." After a long while, she went on to plead her case, "We have some good schools here in New York.

I found it impossible to say aloud what I was thinking: *We have some good schools in North Carolina, also.* I thought it pitiful to have so many thoughts that must be left unsaid.

I was hoping that perhaps she would drop the subject when she said, "I think you would like Hunter's College. Why not go and talk with someone in the registrar's office?"

I thought it funny, as a people, that we did not always say to each other's faces what we appreciated, and what we could not even imagine being without. Maybe we thought of speaking of it as unlucky, or perhaps we saw it as a manifestation of a human weakness we would rather not admit to. Anyway, we knew our hearts. I felt Sister Jason's desire to keep me in the city with her, and I also found it necessary that I try to please her, so I simply said, "Okay."

My New York City mother seemed very pleased. She rose from her chair and said, "Well, tomorrow is a workday. The hour is getting late and we should have been in bed before now. Goodnight," and she started for her room. Suddenly, she stopped in the doorway of her bedroom and called to me, "Mae!"

I answered, "Yes!"

She quickly said, "Registration period is almost over for the Spring semester. You should go to Hunter's College and register as soon as possible."

I called back, "Okay, I'll check it out."

The lady didn't move. I could tell that she had more to say. So, I waited for her to continue. Finally, she asked, "Tomorrow? Why don't you go there after work?"

I swallowed hard, and tried to clear my throat, so that I could answer her. Out of my dry mouth, I heard myself saying, "Of course, I'll go tomorrow after work."

~~~~~~~~~~~~~~

The next morning, as I was on my way to Macy's, I thought of how my existence had been graced with sparks of the unexpected. That afternoon, I would be seeking admission to Hunter's College. It seemed that my chance of attending Winston-Salem Teachers College was slipping away.

When I reached 34th Street, Christmas music was in the air. Songs were also in my heart, as my mind was suddenly jolted to the fabulous Christmas decorations right there before my eyes. My attention was drawn to Macy's windows. There stood Santa, Mrs. Claus and the elves, busy at work in their workshop. Then, there were arctic scenes featuring a family of Polar bears. I stepped inside, and behold, there was a huge Christmas tree decorated with fabulous, colorful ornaments. With all the wonders to behold, I found that there was nothing like

Christmas in New York City. For, I had fallen in love with the
hustle and bustle of the season.

At lunch time, I went downstairs to the bridal department
to take care of the remnants of my duties for the weddings.
Gwen had registered in the department at Macy's, and Sister
Jason had suggested that I select a piece of her china set for her.

I was excited about making my first visit to the bridal
department. The clerks were very friendly and gave me great
service. The beautiful dark, brown-skinned lady guided me to
the bridal book. As I followed her, I thought, *I have never seen a
brown-skinned clerk in a department store, not until I came to New York
that is. It sure feels good to see them.* The lady stopped at a white
book on a table. We sat down. I gave her the names of the
couple, and she turned the pages.

When the names were located, she led the way to the
displayed china. I made my selection from the suggested price
that Sister Jason and I had discussed.

After work, I took the train to the Lenox Hill neighborhood
of Manhattan's Upper East Side. Hunter's College was an
American public university and one of the constituent
organizations of the City Universities of New York.

At the university, I reluctantly had a talked with an
administrator, filled out an application to enter in the spring and
completed a request letter for my transcript from Newbold
Training School in Dover, North Carolina.

On the way home, I picked up a newspaper, and arrived
back safely before dark.

When we had settled into our chairs for dinner, we chatted
about Hunter's College. I suddenly felt more inadequate about
making choices but did let Sister Jason know that I did not want
to work and attend school at night. I had a desire to live in a
dormitory while going to school.

Later, we relaxed while reading the newspaper and some
magazines. Behold, the Little Rock School District issue was
still making headlines. "On December 2, 1957, Minnijean
Brown was taunted by members of a group of white, male

students in the school cafeteria during lunch. She dropped her lunch, a bowl of chili, onto the boys and was suspended for six days."

My heart went out for Minnijean, but I comforted myself with the knowledge that she was not alone in her efforts. God was with her.

~~~~~~~~~~~~~

The wind blew snowflakes in our faces as Sister Jason and I strode forward on our way to church. Going to church three times a week was wearing the Sister down, but she knew how much I desired to play a part in the "coming attraction" as she would call it.

On that particular Sunday, Gwen's sister, Carrie, announced that she had become engaged to the other young man, Patrick, who had joined the church at the same time Arthur had. It seemed that the "coming attraction" had now become a double wedding. Carrie spoke of it as, "God's blessing that had brought them together for a common cause."

As for me, I became overpowered by wonderful feelings. I actually fell in love with love.

Gwen and Carrie Lovett wanted all the attendants to stay after church for a meeting. At the meeting, Carrie, who seemed to be floating on a love cloud, told us about the double wedding. She let us know that nothing was changing except that she and Patrick Owen would join Gwen and Arthur Smith in the ceremony.

Carrie, the prettiest of the three Lovett sisters, was a slender young lady who walked and dressed in model fashion. The mother, Sister Lovett, who was a seamstress, had adjusted and made many of the wedding garments. As the mother of the brides, she was tearful and spoke of the double wedding as a miracle about to happen. She said that she and Mr. Lovett had given the young men their blessings, and Mr. Lovett was feeling honored to be able to walk his daughters down the aisle.

However, Mr. Lovett was not a member of the Church of God, and this particular night was the first time I had seen him.

Years before 1957, Mr. and Mrs. Lovett had traveled North to see relatives. Mr. Lovett was given a job with the transit company—a job that he couldn't resist. They had returned to their native South Carolina Gullah Island briefly, only to retrieve their belongings. Then, the Lovetts had returned to New York City for good.

Still, Mr. and Mrs. Lovett were proud Gullah people. Mrs. Lovett was excited to give us a history lesson about her people. We listened intently as Sister Lovett used her striking Gullah accent, "Gullahs were the people who lived in the area of the Gullah region, extending from the Cape Fear area on the North Carolina coast and going south to South Carolina and Georgia. The Gullah people and their language were also called Geechee and Creole. The language is related to the languages in West African cultures. Gullah crafts, farming and fishing, folk beliefs, music, rice-based cuisine, story-telling traditions, and even witchcraft, exhibit strong influences from Central and West African culture."

The members of the church stood behind the Lovett ladies with delight in the planning of the wedding, and they undertook assigned duties enthusiastically. They were willing and ready to orchestrate the preparations for a double wedding in a few weeks. The date was set for December 22nd. The double wedding would have many attendants from the seven churches.

We were all aware that the weather forecast was not in our favor, but the church congregation was too excited to even listen to weather predictions.

On our way home from church, the silver moon hung in the night sky, while the air was damp and cold from the fallen flakes of snow. Sister Jason was in her quiet mood again, which left me reading Sister Jason's thoughts about the double wedding.

Nothing was said until we were inside our apartment. The lady's face was somber as she said, "I just can't be bothered with foolishness. Those young ladies just want a man—anything in britches."

At first, my eyes avoided hers. My desire for the wedding to take place was already enormous but had grown even greater since the second couple had joined in the celebration. Thank heaven, I had already bought my bridesmaid's dress. I was hoping that the bawdy innuendo was not a suggestion that I should not participate.

Now, I had heard Arthur Smith and Patrick Owen speak, and didn't in any way think of them as 'just wearing britches.' The two guys had been drafted and served together in the colored army. Arthur was from South Carolina, and Patrick was a Mississippian. They both had slight Southern accents and were sho'-nuf good-looking. Feeling well-qualified, they had come North to get skilled jobs in their trades, which they had learned and developed while in service. In their six years, they had traveled near and far, and humbly gave credit to their parents for their hard work, while bringing them up in a segregated south.

When they reached New York City, someway or somehow, they had stumbled upon a bed of roses; however, the roses were a little older than they. In a Southern way, they put on their "grown-up britches" and voiced that "they would hold up their end of the bargain." Thinking of my Daddy, I was thankful for a Southern man. When necessary, Daddy always held up more than his end of the bargain.

Anyway, I had an additional gift to pick up. Picking up Carrie's gift was no problem. Sister Jason and I decided to give her a piece of her china, also. Again, I spent a portion of my lunch period, thumbing through the big, white, bridal book. I turned the pages until I found Carrie Lovett and Patrick Owen. I repeated what I had done for Gwen, and my duty was complete.

The infatuating season brought more snow to the city as it seemed everyone at the New York Church of God, with the possible exception of Sister Jason, was looking forward to the upcoming double wedding.

15 CHAPTER FIFTEEN

MAE

What greater thing is there for two human souls,

than to feel that they are joined for life—to

strengthen each other in all labor, to rest on

each other in all sorrow, to minister to each

other in all pain, to be one with each other

in silent unspeakable memories at the moment

of last parting?

~ George Eliot

The wedding dawned on the afternoon of December 22, 1957. Everyone seemed to be in place: the photographer, brides, grooms, wedding attendants, and of course, the minister.

The church quite literally, overflowed with love, as friends, family, and church members sat to witness the marriages. Guests had come from near and far to celebrate the unions of Gwen and Arthur, and of Carrie and Patrick.

The wedding began with a solo from Evelyn. Her twin sister, Elnora, played the piano, as she did every Sunday.

They both had beautiful voices. Evelyn gave us an extraordinary rendition of "Love is a Splendid Thing."

If we were not already, the song put us all in a loving mood. We, as bridesmaids, were ready to make the introduction of the brides. We were lined up behind the maid-of-honor, according to our height. I stood 5'5", without heels, and was number nine of the twelve bridesmaids. We wore white dresses and carried white floral bouquets. I was so excited and felt good in my white lace dress. As we walked down the aisle, we were each escorted by a groomsman, also dressed in white, wearing a boutonniere of baby's breath.

Gwen wanted her big day to be full of white—a snowball wedding; that was her dream. Now, Carrie said that she would have liked more color, but she was happy to join her sister. Over her lifetime, they had done most things together, and she said, "It was God's plan that they be married at the same time."

When it was time for the brides to appear, a runner was rolled out from where the wedding party stood, to the door. The two flower girls appeared, carrying baskets of white flower petals that were strewn on the runner as they walked. With timing steps, they moved toward the altar. Behind them were two ring bearers. They carried bells, rang them and sang out, "The brides are coming! The brides are coming!"

At that moment, the adults must have thought the children were so daring, sweet and loveable, for there were many smiles, and cheers rang out.

Holding her all white flower bouquet, Gwen appeared down the middle aisle of the church, with her dad by her side. She wore a long-sleeve white lace gown, with a full skirt and long train. The scene down the middle aisle resembled a white winter flower garden.

Glory Hallelujah was in process, until Carrie walked down the aisle with the same dad by her side. She carried a white rose bouquet. She was wearing an elaborate white dress, tightly wrapped around her shapely body with a low-cut neckline. But, it was my guess that Sister Levine had approved of the attire. I must say that Carrie did look darling and daring.

As I stood in front with the wedding party, I could see the shocked faces of some of the Saints of the Church. I looked side-eyed at Sister Jason. She could barely contain herself. Her face carried a sense of disgust.

Both brides wore veils over their faces, which was required by the Church of God.

Elder Boone joined Gwen and Arthur together, as they repeated their vows, held hands and exchanged their rings—sealing the union with a kiss, while sounds of laughter rose up from the audience.

Mr. and Mrs. Arthur Smith held hands and then moved to the side, while Carrie and Patrick stood before the Elder. Looking at Carrie from the back, in that body skimming dress, one could not help but notice the perfect backside. The girl was a show-stopper, and had received much attention, as I had observed. She and Patrick stood side by side and recited their vows. These two spoke louder and firmer than the first couple had when they repeated their vows. They exchanged rings, while the two of them looked at each other with loving, almost daring smiles.

When the moment came for Patrick to salute to his bride, they clung to each other, and lovingly kissed, for what seemed like a long time.

There were different reactions in the audience. Of course, I was happy to entertain the moment, but did feel a tingle in the pit of my stomach. As I looked out over the crowd, I saw smiles, grins, and wry faces, but applause did come from many of the guests.

Sister Jason had an unhappy expression the whole time, so she remained the same old knot on the log—*unmoved*.

As we left the church, the choir softly sang, "How Great Thou Art." Gwen had requested the exit song. As the Saints would say, "Gwen was stronger in the Lord."

~~~~~~~~~~~~~~~~~

The reception was held at a banquet hall in Harlem, which was just a couple of blocks away.

Unfortunately, the weather did not seem to match the radiant glow of the brides. The temperature had fallen below zero, and the snow constantly fell to the earth, while we plowed our way to the hall.

At the banquet hall, round tables were covered with white linens, while vases of white roses and other white flowers sat in the center of each table. The venue already had a lot of color to offer, so the white looked classic. Soft, light music could be heard, but just barely.

The food was light and was nothing like Southern wedding dinners.

An excellent toast came from Mr. Lovett, the father of the brides.

Everyone cheered when the best men gave their speeches about the grooms, and the maids-of-honor gave speeches about the brides. All four of them gave us a glimpse into the lives of the brides and grooms.

Arthur was born and bred in Charleston, South Carolina. His mother and daddy were among the upper Negros of the historical cities of the south. Mrs. Smith was a school teacher, and brought in regular money, and Mr. Smith worked at a cotton factory. Because of their steady work, they were able to survive over the years.

They had three children: one girl and two boys. When the boys were old enough, Mr. Smith took the boys to the cotton factory with him. As, he would pick them up after school. There, they swept and cleaned by his side, without pay from the factory. Their father compensated them, giving each of them hourly rates. Arthur did not care for such work. Over the years, he swore he would quit, if and when, he could find something better, which was impossible in the south.

When Arthur entered high school, he joined the basketball and football teams, and practiced as much as he could to avoid the work at the factory. His father finally let him quit, because he was becoming a stumbling block, rather than a helper. However, he never had as much money as his brother.

His brother, Benjamin, loved his brother and shared his money with him—at times, that is. Now, here at the present time, Ben, Arthur's best man, was here in New York City, telling the story of how Arthur had gone into the Army so that he could assist in sending his sister and him to college, because their parents could not afford to send all three.

Patrick Owen hailed from Mississippi. His first cousin, Troy, was his best man. They were the same age, born days apart, in the same year. In the countryside, they lived hollering distance down the road. He and Troy stayed together, played together, and fought together. Troy's mother was a single parent, who went up to New York, leaving Troy with her mother. There, she got a job and sent money back home to her son. Troy spoke proudly of his mother, when he announced, "Whenever something was sent to me, she would send the same to Patrick."

We all heard the sound of Troy's mother, saying, "Amen!"

Patrick and Troy lived on a farm. Troy said that for the most part, they enjoyed the likes of it. However, even with the hard work, they had very little money. Troy stated that he would never forget how they would bet each other, that one could pick more cotton than the other. Troy said that for the most part, he won the bet. Of course, Patrick wouldn't have that, and argued that he had won the majority of the contests.

The best man went on to say, "Anyhow, Uncle Sam drafted the two of us into the colored army as soon as we were old enough. They split us up, but we kept in touch. And here I am, here in New York City, with my *main* man, Patrick, who got *his-self* a pretty wife."

The crowd cheered, as they toasted the *main* men and

their wives.

At the conclusion of the toasting, the guests enjoyed slices of the two four-tiered wedding cakes. Gwen's featured all-white winter blooms, and Carrie's featured white roses.

The couples had decided to go on their honeymoons when the weather was warmer.

~~~~~~~~~~~~~~~

Three days later, Christmas appeared. Christmas Day was a retreat at Church, with food and Christmas songs. The drama, along with the Christmas music, buoyed my spirit and helped me to focus on the real meaning of Christmas—*Baby Jesus' arrival on earth, and how he later died for our sins.*

The service ended with an inspiring Christmas message from Elder Boone.

Later, when we rode home with the Boones, the conversation was all about the fruitcake that Sister Jason had spent days putting together. The traditional cake was shared with the couple.

When we reached the apartment, the Boones waited, while we made our trek up the steps and into the apartment to retrieve a portion of the cake for them.

Sister Jason cut a good portion, wrapped it in wax paper, and placed the cake in a brown bag. She handed the bag to me, and I took the cake to the waiting couple.

The Boones were very gracious, and, as always, used very pleasant words of thanks.

I smiled and tried to receive the comments with grace. Then, I turned and took the steps up to the apartment, two by two. I was ready for the waiting Christmas Dinner.

16 CHAPTER SIXTEEN

MAE

Education is our passport

to the future,

for tomorrow belongs to the people

who prepare for it today.

~ Malcolm X

Sister Jason was very excited; she had so many plans for us. I was accepted into Hunter's College, for the fall semester, of 1958. In the meantime, I had begun taking a non-credit course, so that I would have a smooth transition. Of course, I was the first in my family to go to college, so there were no traditions, no expectations that I had to live up to. But, I did know that I wanted to succeed.

January was going well. New York City was a white wonderland. The surroundings were something that I had not witness before. My ride on the bus to Hunter's College gave me a chance to observe other parts of the city, and I was in - *ah!* I was truly amazed by the way people could skate on ice without sliding down. I notice some move gracefully over the ice, while some moved slowly. Then there were others who could not move at all.

People were doing many things in the snow. Some of the

younger ones were throwing snowballs. Others were walking their dogs. I even noticed a few little dogs were wearing something that looked like sweaters, and I couldn't believe my eyes.

On January 25th, I became eighteen-years-old. I received many "Happy Birthday" wishes from my co-workers, and we also enjoyed cookies and sodas at lunch time. A couple of people, whom I had met at school, wished me happiness. All and all, I enjoyed the day.

~~~~~~~~~~~~~

Then came the morning of January 28th. The newspaper carried the news on the front page: "ROY CAMPANELLA OF THE DODGERS HAS FRACTURED NECK AS CAR HITS POLE – GLEN COVE, N.Y. Los Angeles' Dodgers catcher, Roy Campanella, suffered a fractured neck early today when his car skidded, overturned and crashed into a pole. His condition was termed critical and an operation was begun."

The next day, the newspaper carried more news about the crash.

"Roy Campanella lived in Glen Cove, New York, on the North Shore of Long Island, while owning a liquor store in Harlem, which he also operated during the baseball off-season and between games. On yesterday, after closing the store for the night, he began his drive to his home in Glen Cove. In route, traveling at about 30 M.P.H., his car (a rented 1957 Chevrolet sedan) hit a patch of ice, skidded into a telephone pole and overturned, breaking Campanella's neck. He fractured the fifth and sixth cervical vertebrae and compressed the spinal cord."

Sister Jason seemed to have known the family quite well. She and I had been to see Campanella play ball, and the thought of his being hurt had put us in a dispirited mood.

As the winter progressed, snow came down like cosmic confetti. I was surprised how happy I was while working and studying at Hunters College. But as I thought of it, studying always made me happy. As I had done in past, I pushed myself for the fun of it all.

All the cold, blistery days passed, and I looked forward to warmer weather.

~~~~~~~~~~~~~

March 1958, came in with the wind swirling around my head as I approached the outside. I had been summoned by the Boones to return a telephone call to my Mom.

With great apprehension, I walked across the street, and knocked on the apartment door.

After I answered their call, "Who is it?" The door buzzed, and I opened the door.

Elder led me to the telephone, and he dialed the number that had been left for me. When the person answered, he handed the phone to me, while he motioned for me to have a seat.

I leaned toward the phone, making sure I could hear.

Mama was probably standing by the payphone, and she answered, "How do!"

With an uneasy anticipation of what might have happened, I asked, "Mama! How you doing? Are you okay?"

"Yeah, I'm well. I just called to tell you that your Uncle Roy was killed when his tractor turned over," Mama said, as if she had to spit it all out at once.

As if I couldn't hear the name, I asked, "Uncle Roy?"

"Uh-huh, your - Uncle - Roy," Mama pronounced it again, slowly and distinctly.

Suddenly, for the first time in my life, I was overwhelmed with a desire to hug my mother. And, I could not reach her.

I thought of Uncle Roy. He had been good to us. He had provided us with transportation quite often. The last time I had seen him was on the day of my high school graduation. Discussing the fact that Uncle Roy was dead put Mama and me in an emotional strain for words.

Not knowing what else to say, I asked, "When is the funeral?"

"Saturday coming," I heard with some sniffles. I had never seen my mother weep, however, there were times that her eyes looked like she had. Then, too, there were times when my grandmother would not let us see her. So, I guess she had wept before, but just now, I could sense it very well. Times like this, let me know that I was surely growing up.

"Do you want me to come home?" I asked.

My Mama whimpered, "Hu-huh, can you come?"

Before I could answer, she had to put additional money into the payphone. I could hear the clinking of the coins. After a couple of minutes, she said, "I'm back."

I really didn't know what to say, but I replied, "I'll talk to Sister Jason about coming home."

Without a sniffle, Mama said, "Let me get off this phone. I've used all the money I have here in my hand. Goodbye!" She hung up.

I sat thinking about Uncle Roy. He was an accomplished black man. When we visited those first cousins, namely, Mae Louise and Martha Ann, we sat in a nicely decorated living room. They also owned a television. Occasionally, we would gather in the plush room and watch "The Amos and Andy Show."

Now, the elderly people in our family were not too keen on such comedy shows, but they did not forbid our watching.

That very minute, Elder Boone, who seemed to have excellent spiritual visibility, came into the room. He asked, "How is the family back at home?"

I said, "Well, my uncle was killed."

Elder Boone showed concern as he sat on the sofa. He asked, "How did that happen?"

Using emotional restraint, I said, "He was on his tractor when it turned over."

The minister said, "Let's say a prayer."

We bowed our heads as he prayed. I listened and took a

look at the big picture and thought matters through. When Elder Boone had finished, uncertainties and confusions no longer weighed me down. As I rose from the chair, I said, "Thank you, Elder Boone." I then took my walk back across the street.

When I reached the apartment, I didn't talk to Sister Jason about going home for the funeral. Instead, I just told her that my Mama had called to tell me that my uncle had gotten killed.

"Oh, my goodness!" Sister Jason lamented.

While she looked on silently, I told her all that had happened.

As all the Saints did, she said, "Let's pray."

We held hands, and silently we prayed.

After we had finished our prayers, I suddenly came to the conclusion that I wasn't going home for the funeral. No matter how much I wanted to be there to hold my cousins' hands, and reassure my Mama, I knew that my Uncle Roy would not have wanted me to let anything prevent me from progressing toward my goal of getting an education.

~~~~~~~~~~~~~~

The first day of the month of April came with showers. This day was known as *April Fools' Day*, and, sometimes, *All Fools' Day*. I didn't play the April Fools' game, and desperately tried to avert the pranks that were played by my co-workers. In early childhood, I was taught that we were not to play pranks on anyone, at any time, not even on the first day of April. My Mama taught us that participating in such mischievous behavior was unethical.

Then came the month of May. The month set aside for honoring mothers. Since I was far away from my mother, I said a prayer for her. Also, on the same day, I received notice that I was accepted at Winston-Salem Teachers College in Winston-Salem, North Carolina.

I suppose, because it was the month of May, I could think

of nothing else but my days back home in the state of North Carolina. I thought of how the greenery lifted its head to the bright sun and blue skies, just after the rainy period of the earth's purification. I could hear the warmer weather calling to me. I guessed the acceptance letter from Winston-Salem had summoned up images of my school days in the south.

The years that I attended elementary and high school, we had celebrated May Day with schools coming together for outdoors activities. The surrounding schools met at Pleasant Hill School on May Day. That particular school had plenty of outdoor space for marble shooting, track, basketball and several May Poles.

Wrapping the May Pole was the dream of my life. The tall poles that were set up, had brightly colored streamers tied at the top. *Months before May Day, we practiced our steps, with a one-two-three, and step. We would go, alternately, right and left of the girls going in the opposite direction, until we had finished the wrapping.*

The rest of the wonderful May Day was spent, cheering the boys onward, as they competed in their activities.

June came to New York City, and the air seemed to be somewhat cool, compared to North Carolina. The semester ended, and I completed my course, *Introduction to Education*, at Hunter's College with flying colors. I was leaning toward going to school in North Carolina in the fall, as Sister Jason wanted me to continue praying on it for a while longer. We had done small talk, but no final decision had materialized.

A few weeks later, on a Saturday morning, while lying in bed with my arms folded against my chest, and staring up at the ceiling, I made an instant decision about what I was going to do next.

I got out of bed and stretched. I was surprised at how well I felt. Why, I had made my decision, and I was feeling good.

Breakfast was sausage, eggs, and toast. As I picked at my food, I am sure that Sister Jason surmised that I had something on my mind. She even seemed to be leaning forward, waiting for me to speak.

I couldn't believe it. I thought breakfast time would be the perfect time to drop my decision right on her lap, but it seemed that I was dumbfounded.

When breakfast was over, we both got up to clean the kitchen. Silence came again, except for the running of the dishwater.

I was thinking so hard, I nearly fell over a chair while I was carrying items to the cupboard.

When the dishes were finally done, I was happy to grab the broom from the closet. With my eyes on the floor, I quickly said, "Sister Jason, I have decided to go to Winston-Salem Teacher's College in the fall."

I did not hear an answer, so I looked up from the floor just in time to see the lady brushing away tears with the back of her hand. She then uttered, "God gave you to me for a while. So, who am I to try to stand in your way? In fact, I could have told you what you were going to do."

The broom fell to the floor, and for the first time, she and I *really* hugged. Tears flowed from our eyes.

~~~~~~~~~~~~~

First thing Monday morning, when I got to work, I stopped in Mr. Langton's office. He maintained the same dress code: suit, white shirt, and a tie. This morning, he was wearing a light gray suit, with an eye-catching tie.

As always, he stood, and asked me to have a seat.

I quietly sat in the chair across from him. Right away, we began having small talk, just as we had done over the months that I had spent at Macy's. The smart looking man had a way of making great conversation and seemed to enjoy the exchange of thoughts and opinions with his employees.

It was nearly work time, so I knew I had to get to the point. I began, "Mr. Langton, I think, I have decided to return to North Carolina to attend Winston-Salem Teachers College in the fall."

"Mae, you did mention that when I first met you, but I really thought you would change your mind, and, maybe, stay a while longer with us," he said, as if he were teasing.

I wanted to make my appreciation known, about my being able to work at Macy's, as I stated, "Really, it was a hard decision to make, Mr. Langton. I do love working here, but I must move on."

Mr. Langton looked at his desk calendar, as he asked, "When are you leaving, Mae?"

Sister Jason and I had discussed a date, and I thought I was ready to spout it out, but saying it was not easy. I stammered, "I- I- will be leaving on the last Friday in July."

He took in a deep breath, while he marked the date on his desk calendar. He then looked up at me, and stated, "You know Mae, I'll miss you, and your quiet disposition. I, also, must say, that you never seemed perturbed about anything. I'm amazed at how you kept your composure when the inventory room had an overflow of work, and a couple of the machines were not in good working condition."

What could I say? *Thank God! I'm just like my mother. I'm pretty calm by nature.* Instead, I smiled, as I thought of: *Beautiful Millie losing her smiling dimples, when a few cards jammed the machine. Susan, the Pepsi drinker, using naughty words when things did not go her way. The union representative, Dan, who was always out of sorts because of some unfair working condition.*

Back in the inventory room, I made my announcement to my co-workers, "I will be going off to college in the fall. I have chosen to go back to North Carolina and attend Winston-Salem Teachers College."

All the workers gave a cheer: "Hurrah!" Even the ones that were under the opinion that I should stay in the city, and also those that had once said, "Going back to the south was like going to *hell.*" They all cheered me on, and Ellen spoke first, "You are very conscientious about your work; so, you should do well in college." Then, Dan, the union representative, who had just delivered a union package, shouted out, "Go on Mae, break a leg!"

A few weeks later, the employees in the inventory department started acting indifferent. Workers went out during the week without announcing where and how the lunch hour would be spent. It was uncharacteristic of the ladies not to share what they had bought when they returned from shopping. Beforehand, they would buy and show the lovely gifts they had bought for someone, who had a birthday, wedding, new baby, or whatever the special occasion might be coming up.

As for me, I didn't shop. They thought it pitiful of me, to buy so little. Sometimes, someone would make a remark about the matter. As my Daddy would say, "It ran off me like water off a duck's back."

Matter of fact, I had bought a few things when I first arrived, but just enough to get by. My desire to go to college was so enormous, I couldn't think of spending my money on anything else. Even if I had wanted to shop, Sister Jason would have been upset to the point that she would have started charging me rent.

On the Friday that I was leaving, Susan and I sat in the workers' lounge at lunchtime, eating our sandwiches. Susan told her naughty jokes, and I pretended that they were funny. The other workers were hiding away, even on my last day of work. I thought, *What do I care?*

When Susan and I returned to the Inventory Department, the door was locked. I looked at Susan, and she stared back at me. I thought, *I'll go where you go.* She looked me, as if to say the same.

Just then, the door flew open. Everyone screamed: "Surprise!"

Even Susan was screaming, "Surprise!"

I was so shocked, I felt lighter than a feather. I went in the room and sat down. The room was almost full of gifts. There were all kinds of goodies on a table on the side.

As always, Ellen was in charge. She acted as the "Mistress of Ceremony." The advisor, department head, and each of my co-workers had their say. All of the talk was exceptionally pleasing.

I had the pleasure of opening the gifts right then and there. I was overwhelmed with amazement when I noticed that I was receiving exactly what I would need to set up a dormitory room. There were sheets, pillow cases, blankets, a bed spread, throw rugs, a trash basket, paper, pencils, scissors, and a few other necessary items. I then understood why they had all disappeared for a few days. The party was well coordinated. I was well aware that when Ellen was in charge of something, it was well done.

17 CHAPTER SEVENTEEN

MAE

The Lord is my shepherd,

I shall not want;

he makes me lie down in green pastures.

He leads me beside still waters;

he restores my soul.

~ Psalms 23:1-2

Sunday morning traffic was heavy, as always, but for me, it seemed to take even longer. We sat in the Boone's car, and to my amazement, Sister Jason wanted to discuss my going off to college. She told how smart I was, and how well I had done at Hunter's College. She announced that I would be taking the Elders' messages to college with me. Therefore, "with my knowledge about the Lord, I would save many."

I squirmed and looked down at the floor.

When I felt my New York Mother's eyes on me, I looked up and smiled.

My happy face seemed to have given her the go-ahead to say more about her Saved Southern daughter. She then reiterated the fact that I had written a number of Elder Boone's sermons in Greg shorthand, typed them, and mailed them to my Mother in North Carolina.

Of course, the Boones knew about this duty I had taken on, and spoke positively about my writing, more than once. They also seemed happy to hear about it, whenever Sister Jason would—*just happen*— to mention it.

When we got to church and went to our usual seats, I was very much aware of the fact that Sister Jason expected a farewell testimony. I was not so naïve as to think that I could get away without testifying, just one more time.

Testimony meeting was opened, and Sister Jason stood when she got a chance. She opened her remarks with the same Bible verse each time she testified. Most of the members were known for a certain verse.

She stood and began: "Create in me a clean heart, O God, and renew a right spirit within me." Psalm 51:10. "First, I'd like to thank the Lord for being Saved, Sanctified, and living a life above sin. Thank the Lord for my wonderful little girl. She came all the way from North Carolina and spent almost a year with me. This year passed so quickly. As most of you all know, she will be going back home to go to college. She didn't promise me that she would stay, but I was hopeful. We prayed and asked the Lord to guide us in our decision making. I know that what she decided is 'God's will.'

Please continue to pray for me, and also for Mae."

After almost a whole year, I still hadn't gotten use to standing and talking to the New Yorkers. I had practiced words as my English teacher had taught me. She had us look in the mirror and rehearse our beginning, ending, and vowel sounds. When we finished Mrs. Rouse's class, we were very cognizant of sounds.

Yet, each time I stood to give a testimony, I would unwittingly block out my surroundings, and would say, mostly, what I had prepared. I did remember that I asked for prayers that God would look over me as I travelled back to North Carolina. At the very end, I said, "Please remember me in your prayers, as I enter into the fall session at Winston-Salem

Teachers College."

On my way out of the Church of God, "fare-thee-well" was said in many ways, so much, that I felt melancholy on my ride home.

I had written Mama, giving her the date of my return. We also shipped the gifts home, along with a few of my belongings.

Sister Jason and I spent the next couple of days putting things together for my trip home. I had my money pinned to my underwear.

Elder and Sister Boone took us to the bus station. The Boones sat in the car while Sister Jason walked inside the station with me. The whole time I was buying my ticket, Sister Jason was sniffling. When I got ready to get on the bus, she followed me to the steps, as her tears flowed like running water.

I was saddened by her tears; and unable to bear the sight, I said a quick, "Good-bye," and hopped on the bus.

After I was seated, I glanced out the window, and could see Sister Jason really weeping. I looked away as the driver made his departure announcement. Then, we drove off.

QUOTES AND QUESTIONS

1. "Many people will walk in and out of your life, but only true friends will leave footprints in your heart."
    ~ Eleanor Roosevelt.

Do you know anyone who has left footprints on your heart? Who are they? Can you find anyone in this novel who was a true friend and left footprints on the heart of others?

2. "You have to get to the point where going for it is more important than winning or losing."
    ~ Arthur Ashe

When you play a game, do you feel that winning is the most important thing? What games were mentioned in this novel?

3. "Ye that love the Lord, hate evil: he preserveth the souls of his Saints: he delivereth them out of the hand of the wicked."
~ Psalms 97:10

Members of some churches are known as "Saints." That is what the church members were known as in this novel. Some people think that the word "Saint" is someone that has died and gone to heaven. What do you think? Why?

4. "The farther backward you can look, the farther forward you can see."

~ **Winston Churchill**

Have you done any research into your ancestry? How far back have you gone? What ideas do you have for the future?

5. "Human progress is neither automatic nor inevitable . . . Every step toward the goal of justice requires sacrifice, suffering, and struggle, the tireless exertions and passionate concern of dedicated individuals."
~ **Dr. Martin Luther King, Jr.**

Have you ever done anything to assist with human progress? What? When? Explain the sacrifice, suffering, and struggle of the individuals mentioned in this novel.

6. "Whoso findeth a wife findeth a good thing, and obtaineth favour of the Lord."
~ **Proverbs 18:22**

Have you found such a favorable situation? Explain. What do you think about the marriages in this novel?

7. "Mistakes are the usual bridge between inexperience and wisdom."

~ **Phyllis Theroux**

Can you recall the characters in this novel who made mistakes?

What were some of the mistakes that were made? Explain the results.

8. "Our greatness has always come from people who expect nothing and take nothing for granted—folks who work hard for what they have, then reach back and help others after them."
~ **Michelle Obama**

Give examples of people in your life and in this novel who "expected nothing, took nothing for granted and reached back and help[ed] others after them."

9. "Teaching is a very noble profession that shapes the character, caliber, and the future of an individual. If the people remember me as a good teacher, that will be the biggest honor for me."
~ **A. P. J. Abdul Kalam**

Tell how you feel about some of your teachers. Discuss some of the teachers that are mentioned in this novel.

.

10. "Live your life while you have it. Life is a splendid gift. There is nothing small in it. For the greatest things grow by God's law out of the smallest. But to live your life, you must discipline it."
~ **Florence Nightingale**

What is the difference between just living life and living life with discipline? Give examples of each. Are there examples in the novel?

11. "The human soul is hungry for beauty; we seek it everywhere—in landscape, music, art, clothes, furniture, gardening, companionship, love, religion, and in ourselves. No one would desire not to be beautiful. When we experience the beautiful, there is a sense of homecoming.
~ John O'Donohue

As a human soul, where do you seek beauty? Name and explain the human souls who sought beauty in this novel. What did they seek?

12. "The courage of life is often a less dramatic spectacle than the courage of a final moment, but it is no less a magnificent mixture of triumph and tragedy. A man does what he must—in spite of personal consequences, in spite of obstacles and dangers and pressures—and that is the basis of all morality."
~ John F. Kennedy

The author of this book feels that this quotation sums-up the theme of the story. What do you think? Why?

BIBLIOGRAPHY

Delany, Sarah and A. Elizabeth Delany with Amy Hearth.

Having   our Say: The Delany Sister's First 100 Years, Bunkyō,

Tokyo, Japan: Kodansha International, 1993.

Newman, John J. and John M. Schmalbach. *United States History:*

Preparing for the Advanced Placement Examination. Revised ed.

Logan, IA: Perfection Learning Publications,   2004.

Portals of Prayers. Concordia Publishing House.

https://www.cph.org/portals/

The King James Version (KJV) *Holy Bible*, Nashville, TN: Thomas

Nelson, Inc., 2003.

Wadelington, Charles W. and Richard F. Knapp. *Charlotte*

Hawkins Brown and Palmer Memorial Institute, Chapel Hill, NC:

University of North Carolina Press, 1999.

Widipedia.org/